Revenge

Also by Mary Morris

Revenge

Mary Morris

St. Martin's Press ⋈ New York

www.stmartins.com

Library of Congress Cataloging-in-Publication Data

Morris, Mary, 1947–
     Revenge / Mary Morris.—1st ed.
         p.   cm.
     ISBN 0-312-32792-7
     EAN 978-0312-32792-7
     1. Women painters—Fiction.   2. Women novelists—Fiction.
     3.   Fathers—Death—Fiction.   4. Writer's block—Fiction.
     5. Stepmothers—Fiction.   6. Revenge—Fiction.   I. Title.

     PS3563.O87445R48 2004
     813'.54—dc22

                                              2004049031

First Edition: October 2004

10   9   8   7   6   5   4   3   2   1

If you wrong us, shall we not revenge?

—William Shakespeare, *The Merchant of Venice*

Revenge

One

It is a fall morning and Andrea is getting ready to set out with her dogs. Opening her window, she takes a deep breath. There is a crispness in the air, the smell of burning. Horse chestnuts are on the ground. Her dogs whine at her feet, anxious to be off, but she ignores them. Today she is not in a hurry. She isn't heading out as the sky is turning pale. Already it is light.

Instead she sits at the window and waits. Looking out, she sees the route she takes every day, past the Vitales' and the Partlows' houses down to the end of Walnut, a woodsy cul-de-sac, where there is a path. The path loops into the woods around a large pond that breeds algae and mosquitoes in summer. In winter children skate on it. In the woods she has seen deer, raccoons, rabbits. Once a coyote darted from of the bushes in front of her.

Andrea loves this cul-de-sac where she lives—Hartwood Springs. It's something about the way the trees drape themselves across the road and the light streaming through them. Now Andrea sits at her window, a cup of coffee in her hand. She is gazing toward the Partlows' house, which is on a rise. If she leans out slightly, she has a full view of the house, with its many wings, the garden, which is a rainbow of mums. Fall blooms.

She can see into the kitchen where Patrick and Loretta Partlow are reading the paper. He zips through the sections as Loretta reads slowly, one article at a time. Loretta pauses to make notes in a notebook beside her. As Andrea takes another sip of coffee, her dogs peer up at her. She pats their heads to calm them down, then looks around her apartment.

Though advertised as a one-bedroom, it is really a single room. A living room, dining room, and kitchen with a sleeping alcove off to one side. In the alcove, her clothes lie scattered on the unmade bed. The radio is on and in the background she hears the news. There is talk of peace in the Middle East, the economy soaring, a scandal that won't go away.

A few of her early paintings hang on the wall. They are mostly landscapes and one portrait of a nude she did in school. She's been meaning to replace them with more recent work but hasn't gotten around to it. Her eyes travel from her paintings to the photograph in the entryway.

It is a picture taken long ago, of a house in autumn, set against a hillside of blazing color. Though it is faded, Andrea can spend hours staring at it. This was their summer house on Shallow Lake. Her stepmother, Elena, sent her the picture just after her father's will was read. It was the only thing Andrea requested from his estate.

Andrea isn't sure who took it, though she believes it was her father. She may have even been with him that day. She hung the photograph in her entryway so that she sees it every time she walks in or leaves. It is the last thing she looks at before she drifts to sleep. Now she gazes at it once more, then turns back to the window.

Patrick is rinsing the coffee cups in the sink as Loretta tosses the newspaper into the recycling bin. It is almost seven-thirty, time for them to head out the door. Normally by now Andrea would have finished her walk and been on her way home. When she walks, Andrea prefers to leave before six-thirty. If she sets out after seven, she runs the risk of crossing paths with Loretta and her husband.

Andrea does not like to have to stop and make small talk with her neighbors or to relinquish her pace. These walks are her only exercise, her time to think. It is on these morning strolls that Andrea tries to make sense out of what happened to her father. She has worn out her brother, Robby. She has worn out several friends, including Gil Marken, the math professor she's been seeing for the past year. No one will listen to her anymore, though Robby in some ways agrees, and Charlie, her former boyfriend, says she may be right but she has no case.

It is true; there is no evidence. Nothing she can prove beyond a series of hunches. Still, Andrea knows what she knows, and though she tries not to think of it, though she says to herself as she walks, "I will think about something else, I will stop dwelling on this," she does not stop. It is as if her mind can find nothing else to settle on. At times she wonders, If I didn't have this to think about, then what would I? She runs it through her mind over and over again. It is a problem, like a Rubik's cube, that she has looked at from every angle, tried to solve, until the pieces began to fall into place.

In the past Andrea went out of her way to avoid the Partlows because Loretta, whom she scarcely knows, would ask in that syrupy voice with the feigned tone of concern: "How is he doing?"

"Is there any improvement? Any change?" Or later, after Andrea's father died, "It was so odd—the way it happened."

She found herself pulling back from these encounters, tightening in the gut. She had a feeling that if she allowed it, this woman would worm her way in. Get under her skin. So she always replied, "Oh, he's the same." Or "Not much change." And she'd watch Loretta's face, the pointy, wily-looking nose, the dark eyebrows that came together, furrowing her brow.

And then, after it was over, after he died, she chose to avoid their questioning stares altogether. It bothered Andrea. The way her neighbor tried to ingratiate herself. After all, Loretta Partlow barely knows her. They know one another well enough to say hello on campus, to exchange cordialities at faculty meetings and greet one another when walking in the woods they share a few miles from the campus.

But when Andrea's father had his accident, Loretta sent a note of concern, an offer to have tea. "Dear Andrea," she wrote, "Patrick and I were so sorry to hear about your father. I can't imagine what it must be like for you. I just want you to know that we are here if you need us . . ." The letter went on for a page or two, talking about losses and the nature of grief, well beyond any other condolence note Andrea received.

"I hardly know her," Andrea said, tossing the note across the breakfast table to Charlie. Charlie works in communications. He publishes the *Hartwood Chronicle*—the newsletter that goes to parents and alumni—and he interviewed Andrea when she first came to Hartwood. He took her head shot as well. Charlie has a good eye for black and white, and Andrea complimented him, saying that his photo of her was her favorite. Afterward they kept running into each other, at the faculty club, at events.

At first Charlie thought Loretta's concern was genuine. "It's a neighborly gesture," he said. But then he asked around. He heard stories about her. A friend once confided in Loretta Partlow that he believed he had been the cause of his mother's suicide. He had left the house one day when his mother begged him to stay, and she had killed herself in his absence. Loretta had comforted the friend, consoled him. She had assured him that his mother was unstable and perhaps would have killed herself no matter what. Then, six months later, a short story with just that plotline appeared in a national publication.

When Charlie heard that, he cautioned Andrea, "Don't tell her a thing. You'll just be grist for her mill."

Andrea had written back—a polite but terse note saying she appreciated the concern, that for the moment she was wrapped up in family matters, but when she had time, in the future, she would let Loretta know.

When Andrea moved into the neighborhood, she wasn't that familiar with the works of Loretta Partlow. She'd read only a novel or two that was required for school, but they hadn't made a lasting impression. But Elena had been amazed when Andrea said she was living down the block from the author of *What If?* "I loved that book," Elena said.

So Andrea read a few of Loretta's early novels, the ones that won prizes and made it to Oprah's Book Club, and a few of the short stories that were always appearing in magazines. It seemed as if she couldn't open a magazine at the doctor's office or beauty salon—or after her father's accident, in the innumerable waiting rooms where she found herself spending her days and nights, and then in lawyer's offices, and outside judge's chambers—and not find a story or poem by Loretta Partlow.

The ubiquitous Loretta Partlow. Like a new vocabulary word, this woman seemed to be everywhere. Her name sprawled across the front of magazines or *The American Review of Books*, where her essays and reviews were published. Or in Hartwood itself, where her knowledgeable and amusing syndicated column, "Gardener's Euonymus," appeared.

Andrea liked the poems best. She found them edgy, often cruel, especially those that explored gender issues. ("His sword cuts through me but I am butter . . ."). She taped a poem to her refrigerator about a man making obscene phone calls to the wrong woman ("For though he did not know me,/it seemed as if he did./He knew where to place his lips;/how long to linger there . . .").

But the novels seemed excessive, and though friends pressed copies into her hands, saying, "You must read this," Andrea could hardly bring herself to finish them. Some were about families, and she could relate to these. A few posed interesting metaphysical questions about the purpose of life, and she thought these were among Loretta's best. But others were grisly and disturbing and focused on extremes of behavior. Not that Andrea wasn't drawn to extremes. But who could think of such things? Women tied down with Velcro straps. Children tormented in unspeakable ways. Though critics said, "Partlow probes the depths of the human psyche," Andrea felt like a voyeur when she read her novels.

When she first met Loretta, who also teaches at the private college where she has long been its most famous faculty person ("Loretta put Hartwood on the map," Gil Marken liked to say), Andrea was surprised. She had expected a large, imposing person. Not this compact, slightly bowlegged creature. Almost a homunculus, a miniature of a woman, "a pocket Venus," Gil called her, and that big, flushed husband of hers, Patrick, who was like a barrel beside her. An overbearing man with sweaty palms and a weak handshake (Her father always said, "A weak handshake is the sign of a weak man") whose true function, everyone knew, was to stand guard between his wife and the world.

But Loretta didn't look as if she needed much protection. Though she was a small woman, petite with sharp features, her fox-like face made no attempt to hide its intelligence. Her eyes were pale blue and piercing, though at the same time revealing little. As if made of glass. She showed her bones—shoulder, elbow, hip— the way a marathon runner might. Her sleek body seemed to point in different directions. Her gray hair (once almost red and considered her best feature) was blunt-cut and usually pulled back into a short ponytail. A broad smile revealed her white teeth.

One day Andrea spotted Loretta running in the woods and found it almost comical to see the woman who had been called "a national treasure" darting on those thin bowed legs, her ponytail bobbing in the wind as if something were chasing her.

From the window Andrea sees them getting ready to leave. Loretta, dressed in powder blue sweats, goes to the patio to stretch. She stretches like a flightless bird, thick in the middle, but with skinny arms and legs. She flaps her arms, bending to touch her toes. She is surprisingly limber, as she curls her head to her knees. She curves her back like punctuation. Andrea has watched her become a parenthesis, an exclamation point, a question mark.

Patrick comes outside with Kippy, their overwrought West Highland terrier. Loretta claps her hands, and the dog leaps up and down, racing in circles at their feet. Patrick pulls a treat from his pocket, and the dog sits as Loretta completes her methodical series of stretches. Then they head toward the towpath, and Andrea gets ready to leave.

She makes her way down the stairs two at a time. The briskness of the day, its clarity, strikes her. She braces for the chill, zipping her jacket. Then dashes with her two mutts, Chief and Pablo, both border-collie-and-something mixes, past the houses of Hartwood Springs to the towpath. The ground is hard underfoot, but the towpath is soft, coated in pine needles, as she jogs along it. The air is so fresh it stings her nostrils. Tears slide down the corners of her eyes.

Andrea slows down and manages to arrive at the loop through the woods just as Loretta and Patrick do. Her dogs bark and growl, racing ahead as Kippy hunches, tail between his legs. Patrick scoops Kippy up, in case the dogs are vicious. Andrea spots Loretta, who has a slightly dismayed look on her face.

Andrea can only imagine what is going through Loretta's mind as they are about to cross paths. She is thinking: there she is—that girl with her green eyes and sad story. That strange business about the father and an accident that may or may not have been an accident.

Though Loretta was once an admirer of Andrea's work, and told her so when she first came to the college, now she would barely know Andrea Geller existed were it not for her story.

But Andrea doesn't really mind. She has begun to suspect that Loretta has a story of her own. Not that anyone really knows it, though her biographers have hinted and her close friends wonder. No one, not even her own husband knows what makes Loretta tick. But in recent months Andrea has made a study of her. She has learned to read between the lines.

In the official story, Loretta grew up outside of Baltimore, a middle child with brothers on either end. In her *Paris Review* interview and in the one approved biography (with the innocuous title *Loretta Partlow: A Writer and Her Work*), she describes her parents as simple working-class people. Andrea saw a photograph of the house where Loretta was raised. It showed a front porch and a black person sitting on the stoop next door. A mixed neighborhood.

But Andrea, who has now read all the monographs, the critical essays and Festschrifts, the unauthorized biography, *Demon Writer*—a book Loretta tried to stop ("rubbish," Patrick calls it)—believes the truth is more complicated. She thinks she has gotten some insight into Loretta's childhood—the father who drank and was known to be violent, who once twisted her left arm (she is left-handed) until it snapped. There is a photo of young Loretta with her arm in a cast. And, the biographer noted, a child with a broken left arm occurs no fewer than seven times in Partlow's fiction, as do many drunken fathers.

Then there are the hands. This Andrea noticed herself. Everywhere in the writing there are hands. Helping hands, hands that tremble, fingers of authority, broken hands. Hands that shake on a bargain, swear to a pledge. Very few hands are held. But many wrists—and faces—are slapped.

Perhaps Loretta made herself a promise when her broken arm healed that she would use it. She would write with it. She'd find the way to get back, the pen being mightier and all. She would pay her father back, and her mother for not leaving him, for staying when she should have gone. It was Loretta who had to leave. She left and never looked back. She was unstoppable. She has been called a diesel engine, a gorgon, a devourer of whatever gets in her way. And this is what Andrea is counting on.

Andrea knows what Loretta thinks when she sees her. It is sad to be someone who is pitied. But Andrea doesn't care. Let her pity me, she thinks. For now. As they approach, Andrea can almost overhear what Loretta is saying behind the hand over her mouth: "There's that girl, the one whose father was in the coma. He had that strange accident . . ."

"Oh," Patrick says, clasping Kippy under his arm. "I thought the college had let her go."

"Oh, not yet. I think they plan to, but she's still around."

"Do you want to avoid her?" He leans in to his wife, touching her sleeve.

"No, she's seen us." Loretta smiles at Andrea, nearing. "It's too late now."

Andrea gives a wave as she reaches them, her cheeks flushed, breathless as if she's been running. "I'm sorry," she says, "I hope they didn't startle you." As her dogs race to the pond,

Patrick puts Kippy back on the ground. "They're friendly, really," Andrea says.

"Andrea," Loretta says, "it's been so long . . . we haven't seen you." She seems pleasantly surprised yet distracted. "I thought you'd moved away."

"No," Andrea says, "I'm still here."

"And you're still at the college?"

Andrea sucks in her breath. She knows this is more a dig at her status than an actual question that requires an answer. She is one of those junior faculty members who just won't, not unless she produces and perhaps not even then, get tenure at Hartwood—a fine liberal arts college (ranked number twenty-one in the country by *U.S. News* & *World Report*). A rural campus just two hours north of the city, which is one of its big draws. One of the most respected women's colleges until the 1960s, when it was forced to go coed. Some people still ask if men are allowed.

Without a growing body of work, Andrea is not the kind of person the college wants to keep around forever, but she is the kind they like to keep around for now, and know they can, for their own purposes. They believe, and they are probably right, that any artist would kill for a job at Hartwood. Andrea is a guest. A long-term guest, it seems, already on her third contract. One who may be overstaying her welcome.

Andrea came to the college with some fanfare, thanks to her mentor and friend, Jim Adler, who hired her for the art department. She was prettier then, with her strawberry-blond hair. There was something spunky about her, though one could already see a darkness in her eyes. But she had worked on a number of series, which had garnered her early acclaim and helped her land the job at Hartwood. All her work involved reenactment (*Backpack*) and repetition (*Dragonfly*).

Loretta herself had praised *Dragonfly*—that multifaceted image with many possibilities but no one true shape—when it was in a Manhattan gallery. She'd admired the glass bricks and the paintings behind them. The play with perception. She told Andrea when they first met that she had been fascinated by the images and found them mysterious and beautiful.

Was it a woman making love? Or being murdered? Or something more banal—perhaps just taking a shower. "And the play on words." Loretta was one of the few people who'd gotten the joke. The contradiction of dragons and flies. The paradox of women who "fly" or, in the face of domesticity, "drag on."

When Jim Adler told Loretta about the new hire, she gave her approval. "She does interesting work," Loretta said. Others had agreed. *Dragonfly*—the conceptual piece about perception and the female body—was compared to Jennifer Bartlett's *Rhapsody* and Judy Chicago's *The Dinner Party*. *The New York Times* described it as "a piece that enlarges our notion of memory and time. Illusion becomes all too real." Critics called it "haunting."

But that was years ago. When her father had his accident, it all came to a grinding halt. Andrea could not work. For years she had no ideas. Now she shifts her feet and tries not to get depressed about her prospects.

"Yes, I have one class this fall," Andrea tells Loretta.

"Oh, that's good. One never knows around here. What with the budget cuts . . . It's hard to predict what the college will do next." Loretta shakes her head, then adjusts a bobby pin in her hair.

Andrea does not want to say that her course load has been cut in half, her benefits severed. That she is furious with the college and looking elsewhere. How she feels they used her and, when she was down, when she had nowhere to go, they cut her off, giving her just one undergraduate drawing class that they had no one to teach.

"Andrea, you know we haven't seen you since——"

Andrea looks at a leaf stuck to her shoe. "Yes, I appreciated your letter. I hope you got my note."

"Oh, yes. You didn't have to. We were so sorry. We've been meaning to have you over. We were talking about it just the other day." Loretta looks straight at Andrea with her pale blue eyes. "And he never . . ."

Always the same question. "No, he never regained consciousness."

"Um." Loretta sighs. "All those years. Well, perhaps it was a blessing."

"A blessing?" Andrea shakes her head. She thinks of her father, lying in his coma. A "head on a bed" was how she'd overheard one resident refer to him—a resident she'd screamed at until hospital security threatened to take away her visiting privileges. Her father who'd always been there for her, who came whenever she called. How could anyone think his death could be a blessing? "No," she says. "I don't think so." Then she whistles for her dogs and walks on.

For years Andrea's routine was the same. She rose early, went for her walk. Then she drove to the nursing home where her father lived. She called it "lived," because he did in fact live there, but not as anyone else did. He was in suspended animation, bobbing on his bed, a man floating. Not Simon Geller, the pediatric cardiologist who had traveled with medical teams to rural China and war-torn Gaza, to the shantytowns of Brazil and the remote parts of Africa to unclog an artery, repair a valve in a child's heart.

This man was a rag doll. Sometimes she lifted his hand only to hear it plop when she put it down. And yet he breathed. He breathed and sometimes he spoke. He said oddly unrelated words such as "spatula" and "fences" and the name of a patient who died long ago. Once in a while he opened his eyes and stared at Andrea as she sat at his bedside. It was always a questioning look, as though he was trying to recall something on the tip of his tongue. A look of wonder at his predicament. She tried to envision the semipermeable state in which he existed, a restless sleeper, moving in and out of his dream.

Andrea had been in her own dreamlike state in the years since his accident. She could not explain the sinking feeling that often came over her. It was as if she had fallen into a dark hole of her own, disappeared into herself. It was more than depression, though clearly it was that. She described it as emptiness. "I'm a cracked vessel," she told her brother Robby.

It was as if she lay in a coma beside him. She went to the hospital, and later, the nursing home, and she sat, watching him sleep. She groomed him. She propped him up in bed and trimmed his hair. She cut his nails, both fingers and toes. Filed them into smooth half-moons.

He gazed at her, almost smiling, as if grateful for the care. He had always been spic-and-span, perfectly clean. Before the accident, if she was going to visit him, she often got her nails done. She shaved him. She liked it when his face was smooth. "There," she said, rubbing her hand across his cheek, "you look nice."

Then one night Andrea woke with a start. She thought she heard someone calling her name. She was trembling, in a cold sweat. For a moment she imagined she was in her father's room and he had actually spoken. An hour later Robby called from San Francisco with "the strangest feeling."

"I know," Andrea said.

On the day of the funeral, Andrea said to Charlie, who has since become her friend, "I heard him call me in the middle of the night. Can you explain that?"

And Charlie just shook his head.

Charlie had come over the night her father had his "accident." She always says it this way. "Accident," making air quotations with her fingers. She never says, "My father was in an accident," because to Andrea it was never just that.

That night remains a blur, a mosaic of time. It was shortly after midnight when Elena called to say Simon was missing. That he had gone out hours before and had not returned.

"What?" Andrea, fuzzy with sleep and perhaps too much booze, asked. She had been out drinking, then suddenly the phone was ringing, waking her. She didn't know where she was. Or how she'd gotten here. "Went out how?"

"He drove," Elena said, her voice rising, "in the car. I don't know where he is."

Andrea shook herself, forced herself awake. "He's driving?" She tried to remember where she was, where she'd been. At a bar in

Poughkeepsie, then somehow she'd gotten home. She touched the bed beside her and felt relieved to find herself alone. She glanced at the digital clock. It was after two A.M.

Her thoughts turned back to her father. "Elena, where did he go?" But in a frenzy, Elena hung up. Andrea's impulse was to jump in the car and look for him, to go searching through the miles of unlit back roads between Hartwood and Poughkeepsie.

Instead she called Charlie. She said, "I'm sorry. I know I'm disturbing you . . ." She started to cry. He thought she was crying about them. They had been seeing each other for over a year and a month before he'd said he was ready for more. He wanted to live together, take it from there. They had argued over that. She wasn't ready. The timing wasn't right.

"I love you," she told him, "but I don't know if I'm in love with you." Even as she said it, she knew it was wrong. It was a distillation of her feelings, not an accurate representation. She struggled to find a way to explain. "I mean, I don't know yet."

"Well, then, you aren't." The hardness in his voice had startled her. "It's pretty simple, isn't it?" Though she'd begged for more time, he couldn't be moved. It surprised Andrea how stubborn he became. He didn't want to see her after that. "I have my pride," he told her.

Of course, that was when she really wanted him. She'd tried to win him back. She showed up at his place with a cake. But he'd just taken the cake, cut them each a piece, and sat at the kitchen table and ate it. She'd been adrift for the month or so without him. Not knowing quite what to do with herself after hours. She'd begun hanging out in bars, drinking too much again. Meeting strange men. Old habits she'd thought were long gone.

But that night Charlie answered her cry for help. He heard her sobbing and said, "Just sit tight. I'll be right there." She sat at the window, listening for his red Honda to speed into Hartwood Springs, pull into her drive. He arrived in a white T-shirt and jeans, a wide, bulky man with a boyish face. A head of dark curls. He came up her walk, tight-lipped, and she clung to him when he stepped in the door.

He was still holding her two hours later when Elena phoned back. They found Simon in his car in the river. A passerby had pulled him out, but he was already unconscious. The police had just come to the house. "Why was he driving?" Andrea shouted at Elena. A man on a delicate balance of Catapres for his blood pressure and Remeron for depression should not have been driving on a foggy night. A doctor who knew how sedating these two medications would be when taken together. He should not have been driving at all.

"You knew his medication," Andrea screamed into the phone. "Why did you let him go?"

"I didn't let him go. He just left," Elena yelled back, then slammed the receiver down.

Charlie went with Andrea to the hospital. He sat with her at her father's side while the doctor explained that perhaps the accident had caused the heart attack, or vice versa. "It's academic," the doctor said. She hated the way the doctor said "academic" without looking her in the eye. What mattered was that her father may or may not wake up, but "probably" he would wake up. In all likelihood, he would. The water had just risen in the car when the passerby saved him. He had not been unconscious that long.

Charlie stayed with her at the hospital day after day as she played her father's favorite music on a CD player. The Beethoven symphonies and concertos. She'd heard that people in comas may respond to stimuli. Favorite tunes, the voice of a loved one calling, as if from the other side of a closed door. She read to her father all of *David Copperfield* and *Mansfield Park* ("He'll die of boredom," Charlie said). She held her father's hand, said his name over and over again.

In the evenings Charlie drove her home. He curled up beside her in bed, holding Andrea while she sobbed. He was drawn back to her. But when he tried to touch her, she pushed him away. "I can't make love with him like this." Charlie made love slowly. He liked the lights on. He wanted to look into her eyes as he stroked her nipples, slipped his finger between her thighs. She couldn't stand it—his lingering touch. She felt exposed. "What is this?" she asked. "A medical exam?"

Though she could not admit it even to herself, Andrea wanted to be taken. With Charlie, there were too many pauses. He held her too long. Caressed her as if he had nothing but time. It made her squirm. She preferred swift strokes, drunken passion, followed by dreamless sleep.

In the two years it had taken her father to die, Charlie became her friend. "He called my name and I heard him," Andrea said, weeping to Charlie on the day of the funeral. "Can you explain that?"

It seemed no one else could explain it, either. Not the nurses or doctors. Not the hospital chaplain. Least of all her stepmother Elena, whom Andrea has not laid eyes on since the funeral. And whom she rarely saw for the two years prior to that at the hospital. "Why is it you're never at the hospital?" Andrea asked.

"It's so hard on me," Elena said, "to see him like that."

"It's hard on all of us," Andrea said. Even before the funeral, Andrea suspected something was wrong. Elena's infrequent visits dwindled down to none at all. Then at the funeral, the way she showed up in a tight black dress and veil, with an odor about her. The smell of drinking. Andrea recognized it right away. Her lipstick smeared. She tottered on her heels.

Andrea had never seen Elena this way before. It was as if some layer had been stripped off and what remained was the cold, hard shell. Even her touch was icy. Robby commented on it as well. "She's a slut," he said.

"Yes," Andrea replied, "but she's not a fool."

Andrea thought there would be tears. Or at least sadness. "She's in shock," said their mother, Barbara, who was not usually sympathetic to Elena. It surprised Andrea that her mother was the only one other than Andrea to cry.

And then there was the aftermath. The funeral over, the reception back at the house near Poughkeepsie. The platters of ham and cheese sandwiches. The potato salads and macaroni salads in metal tubs. Fruit bowls and cookies, all hastily ordered. People standing around with paper plates and plastic forks until Elena suddenly seemed fatigued. "It's been such a long day," she said.

Everyone was oddly silent, unsure of what to do. There was a hurry to clean up. The house a mess, and Elena wanting to straighten up. Scraping plates, putting food away. She seemed to be shoving guests out the door. "Goodbye, Elena," Andrea said, hugging her on the doorstep of her father's house. Even then Andrea remembered that Elena had once given her a clean bed, sandwiches with the crusts cut off.

Elena hugged her back with her soft, fleshy arms and waved as Andrea drove off, then shut the door. And Andrea never saw her, not in person, not even in court, again.

It had taken a year to probate the will, which left the summer house on Shallow Lake as well as the house outside Poughkeepsie (a small place he'd bought after the divorce), all their possessions, and all his holdings to Elena to be distributed at her discretion to his children, Andrea Geller and Robert Geller. After Elena's death the estate was to go to his children. But as long as she was alive, they would get only what she deemed to distribute to them.

It had taken another year to contest the will. Their lawyer assured them that it would never hold. This will was an implausible document. They claimed undue influence. They testified that their father, who was depressed because of his high blood pressure and declining health, could not have been responsible for his actions. Every morning Elena gave him his pills. It was she who dispensed all of his medication.

The judge listened and, in the end, ruled that despite what he thought of the will itself, there was no hard evidence to suggest that Dr. Geller was incompetent. No indication of undue influence. Only circumstantial evidence that, on the face of it, looked questionable but did not add up to proof.

After all, he said, Dr. Geller was a physician, and it seemed unlikely that he did not know what medications he was taking and the effect they would have. There was little the judge could do, because the intentions of the deceased had been made clear, and all previous wills indicated the same thing.

A few weeks after the will was settled, Elena called Andrea and asked if perhaps there wasn't something she would like—some keepsake, some dishes or furniture—something from the house on Shallow Lake, which was already up for sale, as was the house outside Poughkeepsie. She said she was planning to send Andrea and Robby a check as a token of goodwill. "I'm going to send you each five thousand dollars for now," Elena said.

"You can keep the money," Andrea told her (a grand gesture she would later regret), "but I would like the photograph of the house at Shallow Lake."

"Which picture was that?" Elena asked, as if she'd never seen it before.

"The one my father kept in the entryway."

The picture came taped in newspaper and Bubble Wrap, still in its old frame. Andrea unwrapped it and looked at the house for the first time in years. There it was, frozen in time, as if it still belonged to her. She hung the picture where she could always see it in her apartment.

Shortly after the picture arrived, she began to dream about the house on Shallow Lake. She dreamed of it as she saw it from this picture—the expanse of lawn, the screened-in back porch, the long terrace. But in her dreams the house was transformed. There were monsters behind doors, rats scurrying through rooms, barbed wire on the windows. There were rooms she did not know that opened into other rooms and took her to places she had never been.

And then, slowly, she began to work again.

When the phone rings that afternoon, Andrea isn't surprised. She has anticipated the call. She hears Loretta's low but insistent voice inviting her over for cocktails. "You know, after we ran into you today, Patrick and I were talking. We've really hardly seen you, and we feel—"

"But you shouldn't feel badly," Andrea says.

"Please. You must come. Just us," Loretta says, "unless you'd like to bring someone."

"Oh, no," Andrea replies. "That's fine. I'll come alone. But I can't make it today." Even as she says this, Andrea is glancing at her "Galleries of SoHo" wall calendar, which is virtually blank.

"Well, how about tomorrow? Would that be good?"

"Yes," Andrea says, "I think I can make it tomorrow."

Loretta seems relieved. "All right. Shall we say five-thirty?"

"Yes," Andrea says. "That will be fine."

Andrea has been to the Partlows' a few times, but always at parties, in roomfuls of people. Loretta is known for her parties. There is her annual tree trimming, her end-of-school bash, her Labor Day potluck. The cocktail parties she throws when colleagues have books published, when someone receives a promotion or will soon retire. Then there are the spontaneous events she arranges for visiting dignitaries—a head of state from South America, a Nobel laureate from Japan.

It always amazes people that Loretta, with all the demands of her professional life, entertains so often and so well. In Hartwood people say, "I suppose I'll see you at Loretta's on the Fourth." Some of her parties are so much a part of the fabric of the town's life that she doesn't even invite people anymore. They just show up with their sesame noodles, their corn salad. On summer holidays they automatically buy an ornament for Loretta's tree when they are in Prague or Thailand.

It is rare for anyone to refuse an invitation to Loretta's, not to come when summoned. Sometimes friends joke that they're having an audience with her. Loretta is a living legend in Hartwood. In fact, some people have written about her as if she is already dead. She seems like someone who should be.

Loretta has had one of those careers any writer—or any artist, for that matter—would envy. The immediate success with her exquisite first novel, *What If?,* a growing audience with her second, a few spotty years, but then a huge book, *Carnage,* a novel set in France that chronicled the D-day invasion. It won the Pulitzer Prize and made her a best-selling author.

It was praised for "its historic sweep . . . and Partlow's ability to enter the mind of soldiers on the brink of death." Though never stated, it was implied that critics did not see how a woman who really had never been anywhere (before her success, that is) besides Baltimore and Hartwood could imagine the war scenes, the grisly scenarios. But what was most powerful was how she entered the minds of the young men—their preoccupation with wet socks, their girlfriends back home, jobs at the A&P or the steel mill they'd left behind. As one critic wrote, "She seems to channel them."

Loretta spent years researching it along with Patrick, whom she credits for his invaluable assistance. He is also a novelist, though much less successful. He is known more as a literary functionary—a writer who sits on boards, runs programs, judges contests. But Patrick's main job, and this would be how he would describe it, is to protect Loretta. To keep her safe from fans and bad reviews and anything that might impede the engine she is that needs to be fed and spew and can never be satisfied.

So Andrea knows that the invitation is unusual. After all, she's been going past Loretta's for years, but she's hardly ever been over except for a block party and a few artists' receptions. At times Andrea got a piece or two of mail for them. There seemed to be so much mail; mail from all over the world.

She has admired the envelopes of rice paper and blue aerograms with precise, elegant stamps—the feathery cranes of Japan, the rock stars of England, the wildebeests of the Serengeti plain. Stamps, and even letters, she has been tempted to keep. But Andrea returned to Loretta all the handwritten notes from Italy, from Australia, from Singapore.

"This was in my mailbox," Andrea would say, and Loretta would smile a rather timid smile, the kind of held-back way she has of smiling, and extend a frail, almost spindly hand, and take the letter and, after a word or two of politeness, close the door.

The longest Andrea has been inside the house was for what the neighborhood association calls its Moveable Feast, a roving dinner party that goes from house to house. Andrea had just moved in and thought it might be nice to meet the neighbors. A good way to make herself known in the community. "The more people you know around here, the better," said Jim Adler when she began teaching at Hartwood. "You don't want to be the best-kept secret in town. That is, if you plan to stick around."

And Andrea did want to stick around. She wanted to put down roots. Be a part of somewhere, something. So she'd gone. The

Partlows were hosting the appetizer part of the roving meal. Andrea can recall standing on plush carpeting, taking bits of cheese impaled on colored toothpicks from trays that students in white shirts were passing around. She remembers feeling out of place in her navy slacks and light blue turtleneck, an Indian necklace, and fake tortoiseshell clip holding up her hair.

That night on their carpeting, her ankles ached and her body tottered. She had difficulty balancing her wineglass and cocktail plate. She'd left with a headache and a recollection of pale blue and somewhere in a corner, perhaps, a stain, red, like red wine or blood. That was all she remembered of the house, except that she had come home with a vague sense that her life was flawed and other people had what felt like perfection.

Now Andrea stands in front of her full-length mirror, wondering what she should wear. Jeans would be too casual. Certainly not one of the pairs of navy slacks or the long skirts she used to wear. Those got carted off to Goodwill long ago. Shortly after that party, she switched to black. She rifles through her closet, pulls out a few choices—black pants, a black turtleneck.

As she gazes at herself, she is not exactly pleased with what she sees. She is tall and thin, even leggy, men say. Her reddish-blond hair is still thick and curly. But there are dark circles beneath her green eyes, a sunken look in the hollow pockets of her cheeks. Hardly the "knockout" Charlie called her a few years ago. Though she is just thirty-two, there are furrows in her brow. She looks like someone who has not slept, and in fact she hasn't—not that much or that well in years, not without vodka or Seconal or the arms of a man she will never mean that much to. And vice versa.

She tries to comb through her hair so that it isn't so unruly, but it seems to have a mind of its own. Though people say her hair is her best feature, she often wishes she had her father's hair, dark and wavy. A real head of hair, people used to comment. She never looked much like her father, or her mother for that matter, whose black mane was never styled, just pulled back into a ponytail. Some people even asked if she was adopted. Once, in a supermarket, Andrea overheard a woman say to Barbara, "Where did you get her?"

But if one looked closely, it was obvious that Andrea resembled her father a great deal. In the structure of her bones, the squareness of her jaw. In her tight, narrow frame. And anyone who knew them, who saw the father and daughter together—hitting golf balls, skating, playing tennis—saw how alike they were, how fiercely competitive. How hard they fought to prove a point. Or make it. Just to win.

She settles on black slacks, a snug-fitting wintergreen jacket that brings out her eyes. She bought the jacket on a Saturday in autumn several years ago. She and her father had had lunch. They strolled Fifth Avenue. It was chilly, and he offered to buy her a jacket, so they wandered into Bergdorf's. They went up and down the escalators, and she saw them reflected over and over in the mirrors. Her father with his dark hair turning silver and the charcoal windbreaker that set off his eyes.

She tried on jackets—suede, leather, wool, in muted colors. Money was no object. He never looked at the price tag. Her father thought green suited her. A green suede. He examined the snug fit of the jacket, had her turn this way and that. He scrutinized her with his discerning eye. "She'll wear it now," he said, standing beside her, replicated into infinity in the mirrors.

As the salesgirl was clipping off the tags, she leaned close to Andrea and said, "It's nice that your husband takes you shopping like this."

Andrea thrust her hand to her mouth. "That's my father," she said.

"Oh," the salesgirl replied, the color rising to her face. "I just assumed . . . Well, you look so . . . so right together." Then fumbling, trying to recover, "I mean, I see a lot in this neighborhood, you know."

Andrea stands frozen before the mirror. She thinks about changing the jacket, then decides against it. She adds garnet earrings for a drop of color and a smear of wildberry lip gloss. She pinches her cheeks and at five-twenty-five sets out the door.

The Partlows' house sits like a gray spider, built low to the ground, reaching out from its thick, copious center with various arms. It began smaller, with just the belly nestled in a knot of trees, but as success came, extensions were added, with bedrooms off to one side, studies toward the back, a kitchen off another, and a glassed-in porch that doubles as a greenhouse off the back.

It is just a three-minute stroll from her house, and Andrea walks slowly, not wishing to be early or late. She pauses to admire Loretta's garden. It is a rainbow of mums—magenta, pumpkin orange, lemony yellow. There are also Nippon daisies and toad lilies and fall clematis that climbs up trellises, producing a delicate white flower. And some lovely coleus with green and scarlet leaves. Andrea knows this because she has read all of Loretta's essays on gardening. She has sat at her window, identifying the blooms.

At five-thirty sharp she rings the Partlows' bell, and before she has time to take her finger away, as if he is standing behind the door anticipating her ring, Patrick opens the door. He is wearing a red cardigan (cashmere, she notes) and brown corduroys. With a glass already in one hand, he shakes her hand with his free, moist palm. "Andrea," he says, "it's so good to see you."

Andrea smiles, unsure of what to say. They have hardly ever seen each other, yet now it is good to see her. It was one of the things that was difficult for her when she first moved to Hartwood. When people said "We'll give you a call," she actually thought they would. She did not understand that this was a form of politesse, a game to ease one in and out of conversations. But she has learned to play the game as well. "Well," she says, "it's good to see you."

From somewhere in the house she hears the dog barking, as if he has just been set free. Then he runs toward her, yapping louder, his white body bouncing. Andrea stoops down. "Hello, Kippy," she says, rubbing the dog's neck.

"You know his name," Patrick says.

"Yes." She blushes, trying to remember when she first learned it. "I've heard you call him."

He nods, taking her by the elbow and leading her inside. "I'm sorry. We really should have had you over sooner."

"It's all right. I've been busy myself."

Andrea follows him into a very tidy house with an expansive living room and huge picture windows overlooking Loretta's garden and the meadows and the pond Andrea walks around with her dogs.

The room she enters is done in pale blue, both walls and curtains, as if intended to match Loretta's eyes. The furniture is a slightly lighter shade of blue, and the bookcases are painted white.

She has never been alone in this room before and is surprised by how big it is. How open. There are so many things in it—so many books and paintings, glass sculptures, places to sit and read. Yet it doesn't seem cluttered at all. The carpeting feels as if she is walking inside a cloud. Patrick goes to a panel and flicks a switch, and the venetian blinds open, bringing in more light. "Passive solar," he says, pointing to the panel, "but you can override it." Andrea blinks at the passive solar panel, then gazes back across the room.

It is brighter now, and she can see that the walls are lined in shelves, rows and rows of books, all in alphabetical order by category. Fiction, nonfiction, poetry, travel. Hundreds, thousands of books. On the table are bowls of olives, mixed nuts, mozzarella sliced with sun-dried tomatoes. A basket with crackers and bread. "Please, come in, have a seat. What would you like? White, red, or something stronger?"

Andrea contemplates, then decides against something stronger. "Oh, white would be fine."

Patrick disappears into the kitchen, and Andrea is left alone. The music of an easy-listening CD fills the room. Andrea identifies it as Brubeck. She fiddles with her pants, her shirt. She thinks she hasn't dressed properly. Her jacket doesn't quite fit her anymore—it feels too tight—but she is reluctant to give it away. Still, she fears it will buckle when she sits down.

Not knowing what else to do with herself while she waits, Andrea scans the walls. The books, the pictures of Loretta Partlow with other famous novelists, mostly male, two Nobel laureates. Loretta receiving an American Writer's Award. A medal from the White House and a picture of Loretta shaking hands with Bill Clinton. A few photos of Loretta and Patrick, smiling at some event. And on the glass table near the sofa, some family pictures: Loretta holding a baby. And later, a picture of them with a boy.

Andrea has heard that they had one child who used to be seen riding around Hartwood on a bicycle in winter wearing just a flannel shirt. Once, when Charlie was in high school, he babysat the boy and said he used to fend for himself, scavenging in the kitchen, opening cans. The boy, who'd left Hartwood years ago, rarely returned, and most people considered him estranged. There are only a few pictures of him, and they all seem to be from when he was very young. One or two appeared posed, not the usual pictures taken on a boat, a reunion, at a country fair.

Andrea has drawers full of these—loose snapshots of her family fishing on the lake, on a picnic, in front of the Leaning Tower of Pisa. The pyramids of Mexico. She has albums and boxes that her mother gave her of them doing this and that, not happily, really, always in some kind of conflict, some problem or issue, some fight, something her parents couldn't get along about, but they were a family. At least until Elena came along, they were. They did things together. There were pictures—evidence—to prove it.

When Patrick returns with the wine, Andrea looks up quickly, through the vast expanse of living room. "This is lovely," she says, gazing at the space around her and already feeling her own flawed life enveloping her. "It's so . . . so blue . . . so big."

"Oh, we love it. We love to just sit at this window and look out at the woods and the pond."

"You do have a good view," Andrea says, rising on her tiptoes.

"You know, we never want to go anywhere."

"I can imagine. It's like heaven."

"What's like heaven?" Loretta asks, emerging into the room from, Andrea assumes, her study off to the side.

"All of this." Andrea makes a sweep of her hand.

"Yes, I suppose it is." Loretta is wearing black slacks and a pink angora sweater. Her glasses hang from a gold chain around her neck, and except for the glass of white wine in her hand, she looks like a guidance counselor from the 1950s. *Our Miss Brooks,* a show Andrea's father liked to watch reruns of. Prim, even priggish, with her gray hair pulled back from her face, leaving Andrea with a sense that she is paying a visit to her elderly aunt. "We never want to leave, do we dear?" She turns to Patrick, who gives her a nod. "But we have to go places all the time."

Patrick shrugs. "You could say no, I suppose."

Loretta shakes her head. "It's hard when people invite you year after year. Sometimes it seems as hard to turn them down as it does to go. We just refused an invitation to China for the second time." She sighs. "They seemed so disappointed. They said they'll ask us again next year."

"You'll have to say no again," Patrick teases her.

"I'd actually be interested in going. There's so much happening in China now, but it's such a long trip. Anyway, let's sit down." Loretta settles into the sofa, and Kippy jumps up after her. "Do you mind the dog?"

"Oh, not at all," Andrea says.

Loretta pats the place beside her. "Here, sit next to me. So, how are things for you? At the college and all."

Andrea sits down and sinks into the sofa. She keeps sinking and for a moment feels as if she will keep going to some dark place deep in the earth. She fears she might disappear altogether, and then she settles. "I'm quite busy. I have a new painting studio this term and—"

"I've heard about those cutbacks in the art department. It's a shame, really. I hope it doesn't affect you."

"Oh, no," Andrea says, lying. She finds her spirits sinking as her body did. She feels caught in this sofa and in Loretta's stare. Andrea wants to talk about her new studio, a place that has become a kind of sanctuary for her. How she can go there anytime, night or day, and lose herself in her work, which, of late, has consisted of a series of paintings. How she is glad that the college has given her this space. She wants to talk about all the new work she plans to generate from this studio. What she does not want to talk about is the reduction in her course load, the slashing of her benefits. "I've got plenty to do."

"I'm sure you do. How are your students?"

Andrea has the impression that she must talk quickly if she is to answer the questions being posed, because Loretta is already ahead of her, moving on to the next thing. "They're good, but you know, I feel as if you can teach drawing to anyone."

"Really?" Loretta says, taking this in. "I don't think I could learn."

"I think anyone can. It's just a matter of perception, really. Learning how to see."

Loretta seems to be pondering this. "I read once that Jackson Pollock could draw very well. It's hard to believe."

"Yes, I've heard that, too."

"So your new paintings, what are they like? I remember that early piece . . ."

"*Dragonfly*. That was a long time ago." Andrea says this with a laugh. She can envision *Dragonfly* in her storage locker, the neatly labeled cardboard boxes where it has been sitting for years. "I've been working on a new series for a little while. It's a group of realistic miniatures, almost photorealism, but with surreal elements thrown in." Andrea shakes her head. "It's hard to describe." But she smiles as she thinks of it. For the past few months she has returned to the studio working late into the night, sometimes not eating, at a manic pace.

"I think Jim Adler mentioned this to me." Loretta cocks her head as if trying to recall a conversation. "He said your new work is quite good."

Andrea feels buoyed that her mentor and friend, Jim Adler, who stops by her studio from time to time to check on her, would share his opinion with Loretta about her work. "That's nice to know. This new series, it's of a house my father built."

"He built it?"

"He had it built. On a lake."

"You must show me the paintings sometime. I remember *Dragonfly* very well. I'm interested in young artists . . . You know, I was so sorry to hear about your father. I've been meaning to give you a call," Loretta says, that look of concern coming over her face. "It's strange that we can be neighbors, teach at the same college, and know so little about each other. But I'm sure it's been hard." Her eyes narrow, giving her a ferretlike quality.

"Oh, it was, though it's been a while. But it has been hard."

"Yes, I know. The circumstances . . ."

"Well," Andrea can't quite stay focused on what she wants to say. "Yes, the circumstances were . . . strange."

"I'd heard something about that."

Andrea struggles to go on. "But the worst part for me has been . . ." She finds it difficult to continue and takes a sip of wine. Though she thought she was past the point of breaking down, now she isn't so sure. "My father and I were very close."

"That must be particularly difficult."

"Yes, he was the one person I could really count on."

Loretta nods, then turns away. She seems to set her gaze on the picture of her son on the glass table behind Andrea.

Andrea continues, "He really believed in me. That was the main thing."

"It must have been good to have had such a supportive father."

Andrea nods, feeling the enormity of her loss. "It was." She sighs. Even as she says it, she thinks about how her father was always there for her. Much more of a presence than her mother, who was so distracted. He was Andrea's lifeline. In his suit and tie, with his mustache trimmed. Camel-hair coats and fedoras. Even in khakis and a cardigan (always cashmere, like Patrick, she notes), a man who knew how to dress, how to present himself. A dapper man. But still, he was always there for her "messiness." There to bail her out when she went astray, which happened from time to time. In the difficult years, when her parents separated and then divorced. And afterward, when she needed help. When she'd struggled with alcohol and drugs.

"It must be especially hard," Loretta says, leaning forward almost touching Andrea's hand. "If you were so close, with the accident . . ."

"Yes, they called it an accident, but to be honest, I've never been satisfied with that explanation. I've never quite believed it."

"You mean . . ."

"I don't mean that someone drove him off the bridge. But he never should have been driving. That much I can say for a fact."

"What do they think? Did they ever determine the cause?"

Andrea feels a kind of heat surrounding her. A rage she has never been very good at keeping in check. He should not have been driving. He never should have been at the wheel. Everyone knew that. Elena more than anyone. Why was he alone? Where was he going? And what was on that slip of paper the police found in his hand, the one they confiscated, then somehow misplaced, the one that was never found?

A shopping list? For years Andrea has tried to imagine the words, scribbled on a notepad, soaked in the river as the waters rose. *Eggs, milk, beer. Bananas.* A confused man going on an errand at nine o'clock at night?

She has tried to reconcile these things—her father's illness, his driving off the bridge. The illegible note. She says, "It has been declared an accident. The case is closed. But not in my mind." Andrea sips her wine, then turns to Loretta. "Would it be all right if we don't discuss this? It's very painful to me."

"Oh, we are so sorry," Patrick says. He gazes at his wife with a look of concern. "Perhaps . . ."

Andrea feels the tears. Real tears welling up in her eyes. "I'm sorry," she says, "I think I have to go."

"Of course, my dear," Loretta says, obviously surprised by Andrea's sudden emotion. She takes a sip of wine and rubs the wet spot where the wineglass sat as Andrea collects herself. "So," Loretta clears her throat, shifting her legs beneath her, "are you friendly with any of the neighbors?"

Andrea is relieved by the change of subject. "Just the Romanellis. They're very sweet. I mean, they're simple people, but . . ."

"You rent from them, don't you? We've lived here for years, but we hardly know them. We're good friends with the Vitales. He used to be head of Romance languages. Do you know them?"

Andrea shakes her head. "Just to say hello."

"Well," Loretta says, patting Andrea's knee, glancing at Patrick, "we'll have you over with them sometime, won't we, dear." Patrick gives his wife a nod.

"I'd like that," Andrea says, glancing at her watch. "I should go," she says, getting up, "it's getting late." At the door Loretta gives Andrea a hug that surprises her. Patrick does, too. Then she says good night and walks home.

That evening, before she goes to bed, Andrea opens her window and looks up at the stars. It is a clear night and the air is fresh with the hint of fall. Normally, when Andrea looks out at night, she gazes into an abyss of darkness, but tonight as she looks across Hartwood Springs, every house is dark except for the Partlows'. A single light glows from one of the wings.

———

It was right after the will was read that Andrea began poring over the collected works of Loretta Partlow. It had begun inadvertently at first, as a way to occupy herself, to pass the time while she waited for her father to awake. It helped her to read about the miserable lives of other people. Once, in an airport, Andrea paused at a rack of paperbacks, turning it slowly, and said to herself, "I want to take all my suffering and put it right there."

She could see Elena on her way somewhere. Just having finished a book she was reading, pausing at a rack like this one. Browsing. Elena would pick up a title that intrigued her and, perhaps standing there, or better, on an airplane, a long flight somewhere—Paris or Singapore—in a middle seat, where there was nowhere to go, she would begin to read. At first it would not sound familiar, but soon the story would begin to resonate in her mind. In Andrea's fantasy, the narrative grows more complex. Elena is in a book group and they have assigned this title. Not only would she be on the flight, reading it, but later, having to face her friends, who live in their gated communities in Newport Beach, Leisure World—the wives of successful men, who swap ideas on the tennis court or beauty salons, who would all greet Elena with, "Didn't your husband have an accident like this?" "Wasn't he a cardiologist, too?"

It was common knowledge that the famous novelist lived at the end of Andrea's street. When she first moved in, Andrea had seen her, walking her white dog in the woods, but she knew little about her. Then one day as she roamed in the hospital, waiting for her father to wake up and get on with his life, Andrea found a copy of *Harper's* with a story by Loretta Partlow—a story entitled "The Dead Spot" about a couple who go sailing. The man, who is debating whether or not to leave his wife, accidentally kills her. This time, perhaps because of what was happening in her own life, Andrea found it riveting.

Except for what she must read for her classes, she has read nothing besides Loretta Partlow since. At first she read the books and stories, essays and poems, in a haphazard fashion, without paying much attention to order or sequence. She read whatever she found lying around. She dug up the books friends had loaned her, which she'd never returned. She read the novels that had been nominated for prizes and the two that had won them, though long ago, early in Loretta Partlow's career. Slowly the reading took on a life of its own.

Like a biographer, Andrea set herself the task of reading the whole body of work in the order in which it was written. And there was so much. So many books and articles, short stories and poems. The nature essays and a sentimental volume on gardening called *Snippets and Cuttings*, in which Loretta compared gardening to writing: "A gardener, like the writer, learns you can take anything out, you can move things around."

And there was the more offbeat work—a coffee-table book on arcade freaks and an extended essay on the impact of silent films entitled "The Right to Remain Silent." It seemed there was nothing that could not entice Loretta's curiosity. Her omnivorous interests extended to baseball and art history. Her essay "The Captured Moment in Vermeer" was now a staple on Andrea's syllabus.

While Loretta is capable of poignant stories of childhood and growing up, such as *Signs of Life*, in which a boy grapples with his father's suicide (it is a book Andrea now loves), it is her Gothic works that have made her famous. And rich. She is known for her ghoulish imagination, her flair for the strange and bizarre. The woman who sets out to understand her brother's death only to realize she knew nothing of his life. The private investigator who comes to understand that the person he has been seeking is himself. Loretta seems to have an endless fascination with forensics, detective work, discovery.

While reading the books in order, Andrea made discoveries on her own. She found it instructive, for example, to read the books of poems that preceded specific novels. Loretta seemed to be working out certain themes that she would in turn dramatize in her novels—themes such as the family, gender and sexuality, notions of power, lost love, betrayal, man versus nature, mortality.

In all the writing, Andrea found a kind of perversity—fetishes, genital fixations, mutilations. In most of Loretta's work, there was violence, but also a kind of ironic humor. Andrea concluded that what Loretta was writing about most was madness. And obsession.

But there was a period of about ten years when Loretta seemed to write her darkest tales—stories of captives, girls locked in root cellars, disappearances, drownings, racial violence of the cruelest sort, unimaginable torture and perversions. Things that would be difficult for anyone to dream up. It was as if she had taken the tabloids and turned them into fictive tales. Yet some were deeply compelling. And others disturbing. Some were brilliantly written; others felt dashed off, as if Loretta simply couldn't *not* write them.

Then, a few years ago, Loretta seemed to have emerged from this darkness. The stories became lighter, the themes more everday. Teenagers morphed from sadist gang members into college students majoring in accounting. Lost children reconciled with parents with the help of their ministers. Bad marriages that once ended in murder finished in the tedium of divorce. Couples found ways to stay together through therapy and hobbies such as bird-watching.

None of this latter work made much sense to Andrea, who had inadvertently become a student of it. Some critics wrote that Loretta Partlow stopped being a madwoman herself and returned to more traditional fiction, but Andrea was left with a different feeling. It did not seem possible that the woman who had gone through these ten dark years could emerge to craft such normal stories of daily life. It seemed to Andrea that there was no way back from the dark journey Loretta had embarked upon.

It occurs to Andrea that the stories Loretta Partlow had published in recent years were in fact written long ago. Loretta hasn't written anything new in a while. Perhaps, Andrea speculates, it has to do with her son. Or maybe she is just an artist hitting a wall.

But this does not really matter to Andrea. Because she's begun to imagine a story of her own unfolding.

Her father's house was filled with the smells of roasting chicken, creamed corn, mashed potatoes, green beans, and biscuits. Rich, buttery smells. Andrea could not remember ever smelling so many things at once. Her father had picked her and Robby up from school, told them he was bringing a woman to dinner. But the woman was already in the kitchen when they got there.

She had an apron on and was stirring a pot, tasting something with a spoon. Simple gestures Andrea had rarely seen performed. The woman was short and fleshy, but she had big amber eyes with colored flecks, like ponds in summer. "So there you are," the woman said when they walked in.

It was a meal intended to seduce small children, with the potatoes whipped to a froth, the chicken crisp and brown; but though he was three years younger than Andrea who'd just turned twelve, Robby was not impressed. He whispered into Andrea's ear, "She knows where everything is."

Robby was right. They had not noticed this stranger settling herself into their lives on the off days when they lived with their mother. They hadn't seen the string of cultured pearls left in the soap dish, the bottle of lavender shampoo. The slippers by the side of the bed. They had, at times before their parents separated, awakened in the night to shouts and accusations. Andrea had heard their father, a scientific man, say, "But what is this based on? Where is the proof?"

Their parents met in grad school. He was on his way to medical school and she to a career in research. This was how they always spoke to each other. With the kind of directness, the frontal attack, of scientists and probers. They were always asking each other, and their children, for the facts, the truth. If Andrea got a B on a test, her mother had to know the percentage of the class that also got B's and exactly where Andrea had gone wrong.

There could be no ambiguities, no shades of gray. So when their mother began to suspect, when she began to feel that something was wrong but she could never say what, no one believed her. She didn't even believe herself.

It wasn't until Andrea smelled the meal Elena had prepared that she understood this other woman existed. Perhaps she had existed for some time. But still, as she ate dreamily, Andrea, thinking of the TV dinners, the canned vegetables, and the macaroni her mother served, replied like some kind of traitor to her brother's accusatory tone, "It's better than what Mom makes us."

She watched her father leaning over his food, laughing. The way he pushed himself away from the table when he was done. How long had this woman been in his life? After dinner, when the dishes were washed, he drove Elena home, but he was away a long time. The next time they saw her, he did not bother driving her home. Still, everyone was astonished when he married her. She seemed so different than he was. He was a cardiologist at Albany General, and she was a secretary in admitting. She was dark and strong, from "out west" somewhere, she'd say with a flick of her wrist and a laugh.

It was a love of books that had brought them together. He had seen her in the cafeteria, absorbed in a novel he'd long admired, and soon they were talking books, swapping them. But while her father read them and discussed them with his book group, Elena seemed to consume them. She read with a concentration that was frightening. If you interrupted her, she would give you a dazed look that could turn into an outburst. It was the only time she ever seemed capable of true rage. She even said once, "Don't you under-stand that when I'm reading, I'm not really here?"

Elena read whatever she put her hands on, whatever she heard mentioned on the radio or in a newspaper—not as a sign of her intelligence really but more as an indication of her ability to trans-port herself. She was capable of getting up in the morning and reading all day. She easily finished a book in a sitting, and she never put one down once she'd picked it up. She read classics and trash and did not seem to discriminate between them as long as there was a story she could get caught up in. When a character died, she went into mourning. A triumph became her own. But family friends were dubious. Elena seemed to have sprung from nowhere. A forty-year-old woman without a past. It was a rebound, people said, though she gave Simon and the children the kind of structure and routine he craved. Barbara, the research scientist, never had time to put a meal on the table or sew a torn pant leg. She never made it to assemblies or cleaned her children's rooms. Her life revolved around petri dishes and stem cells. It was difficult to compete for the time of a mother who was set upon curing incurable disease.

Elena worked her way into everyone's hearts, starting with the children who grew fond of her. She waited for them after school. She had made funny snacks on platters for when they walked in. She called the snacks her geometry lessons—triangular sandwiches of salmon and cheese, sliced circles of peanut butter and banana, cookies cut in squares. "So what will it be today, children?" she'd ask as they left for school when Simon still had joint custody. "Circles, triangles, or squares?"

It was true she made changes, especially to the house on Shallow Lake. She put out lawn gnomes—leprechauns reclining under trees, and two "little Negroes," as she called them, one dressed as a butler, another pushing a wheelbarrow that she liked to put a flowerpot in, until Simon made her take them down. Robby referred to her as "the weirdo."

But she gave to Andrea what her mother never had. Hot meals on the table, clean warm beds, clothes that had buttons, matching socks. Elena was small and round, and you could put your arms around her. She was so different from Barbara, who was more at ease in a lab than in her own home. And from Simon's mother—a cold, demanding woman wrapped up in herself. Once, when Andrea was in college, Elena turned to her and said, "You know, I don't think your father ever got over his own mother until he married me."

And Andrea had agreed.

Two

The letter is in Andrea's mailbox the next day. Handwritten, without a stamp, on a sheet of personalized stationery. Loretta must have slipped it into the mailbox that morning. "Dear Andrea, I am afraid that I upset you last night, which wasn't my intention. I didn't mean to pry or open old wounds, but if you ever want to talk, if you ever need a friend, well, you know where I am. Please don't hesitate. And we'll have you over again soon. Warmest regards, Loretta."

Andrea takes the letter inside and puts it in a drawer where she keeps important things: documents—including her father's accident report and his autopsy report—special letters, among them a packet to lawyers and legal advisers; long handwritten letters to Elena, never sent; and family pictures, including a snapshot of Simon, Andrea, and Robby fishing.

Andrea isn't sure when she will respond to Loretta's letter. Or how. She is not in a rush. She has been patient this long. She can wait a little longer. Besides, it is Tuesday, a busy day, when she teaches her studio class. She takes the dogs for a long morning run. Then she leaves a note for Mrs. Romanelli, asking her to let them out if Andrea isn't home by dark, something Mrs. Romanelli doesn't seem to mind doing.

Andrea rents the upper floor of a two-story house from the elderly couple who live downstairs. Andrea has lived in many places over the years. She rented an abandoned church when she first moved to Hartwood. She has lived in a boat and above a garage. But she's rarely lived in a house since she got out of art school. She hadn't wanted to.

Houses reminded her of things. Of Sunday afternoons and family outings, of birthday cakes and setting the table. But in the past few years, a house—or at least an apartment in someone else's house—has come to please her. It gives her a sense of settling down. Of her life taking on some heft, some weight. She's almost part of a family, even one separated by walls and doors, to whom she pays rent.

The Romanellis are easy to get along with, though noise does bother them. They were understanding when she got the dogs from the animal shelter over a year ago. "I need something," she confided in Mrs. Romanelli when she asked if she could get them. "Some company."

"But no noise," the older woman said.

Andrea had to carpet her floor, but this has been the least of her worries. Not many of the homeowners who live in the cul-de-sac are happy about the renters who live in some of the upstairs apartments of these family homes where kids went off to college and never returned. There are perhaps only four or five renters, but the owners' association fought to keep the tenants out, and Patrick Partlow was one of the strongest voices against them.

Hartwood Springs is, after all, a stable upscale neighborhood beside the college town of Hartwood. Hartwood itself consists of one main street with an independent bookstore, two coffee bars, a stationery shop, a sporting-goods store, a pizzeria, and a lingerie shop that has resisted moving to the mall. It is a medium-size city of students, adjunct professors, and townies, most of whom work for the college.

In the past few years the college—a tuition-driven institution with a relatively small endowment—has been quietly granting tenure to fewer and fewer faculty, letting tenure lines go altogether, and bringing in more part-time help. Everyone knows what this is about—no benefits, no health insurance, no pensions. It is an issue in all the departments, and Hartwood Springs, which several long-term tenured faculty members call home, does not want transients living in their midst.

Andrea came to the college four years ago, on a guest contract to replace Jim Adler, who was then a retiring professor of art. Years ago Andrea had written him an admiring letter, speaking of his early work, his black-and-white geometrics. He had written back saying he had seen her *Dragonfly* in a SoHo gallery and was impressed. Andrea had tried to convince a curator friend at the Whitney to do a Jim Adler retrospective, and she told him so in her next letter. Though that had never come to be, when he was thinking about retiring (though he has yet to actually do so), Jim Adler recommended Andrea for a guest appointment until Hartwood was ready to do a search for his replacement.

Though Andrea knew most working artists would do anything

for a job like that at Hartwood, it had been hard for her to leave New York City and her Brooklyn studio. At first she contemplated commuting, but Jim told her it would be best if she tried to settle in. Be part of the community. He assured her the job could easily turn into tenure-track once he officially retired.

Neither of them knew that Jim would remain as long as he did, or that the college intended to let the line go anyway and just keep guest faculty. But jobs were hard to come by, and it wasn't that far from the city. Or from home, for that matter. When Robby heard about the offer, he didn't hesitate. "Take it," he said. Six months later, when their father had his accident, she was glad she had.

She'd taken it and found housing on the top floor of the Romanellis' house—an apartment they had been saving for a daughter who had moved to Seattle and wouldn't be needing it. The Romanellis ran a bakery in town and had lived there before people began buying houses around Hartwood Springs, buying them to tear down and rebuild because the land near the pond, which was more of a lake, was desirable.

Soon everyone around the Romanellis had sold, and new houses in the cul-de-sac were built, houses that looked too big for their lots, though most had a shield of trees and shrubs. The Romanellis had held out, though their house was dilapidated by anyone's standards—the front porch sagging, the pillars badly in need of paint, as was the house itself. Even from the road, you could see the torn screens, the attic window held together with duct tape.

For a time people made comments to Andrea. They said that the Romanellis weren't house-proud; that their home was an eyesore. But Andrea didn't mind the run-down state of the Romanellis' house. It rather matched her state of mind—not quite tidy. Improvised.

Her own life had a makeshift, slapped-together feel, so this house suited her.

Besides, the Romanellis were nice. Mrs. Romanelli brought Andrea lasagna. They didn't mind the dogs once Andrea put the carpeting down. But Andrea didn't realize until well after she moved in that some neighbors, including the Partlows, were actively trying to have her evicted.

At first she was angry about this, but by then she had other things to think about—the care of her father and waiting to see if he would revive. And then there was Elena and the way she stopped showing up, the way Simon didn't seem to matter to her. These preoccupations had taken Andrea over, so she put aside all the little squabbles and local politics. She had hardly concerned herself with the Partlows or the neighborhood association.

A few months after her father died and Andrea began reading the works of her famous neighbor, she had a dream about Loretta. Until then she hadn't given her much thought. In the dream Loretta Partlow took the form of a praying mantis with those piercing blue eyes, and it was flying around Andrea's room.

In her dream Andrea was terrified, but for some reason she pulled back the covers and spread her legs and the praying mantis, known for eating the heads of its mates, nestled in the warmth between her thighs. Andrea woke with a tingling that coursed through her and was not unpleasant. She thought she'd had an orgasm in her sleep.

A few nights later, Andrea knew what she was going to do. It wasn't a plan exactly. It was more like an idea that unfolded slowly in her mind. It didn't take shape all at once, but rather like a garden, a kind of work in progress, it grew one piece at a time. Then one day there it was, planted, taking root.

Fifteen students stare at the naked male figure before them. Though it is their third class, Andrea has yet to learn their names. She thinks the girl with the blue hair and the rings all up and down her ears is Beth, but she isn't certain. It may be Dawn. The boy who draws fairly well, she's pretty sure, is Marc. The rest of her students come to her as a sea of faces when she tries to pin each one down to some particular aspect of his or her anatomy or character.

Today the focus will be on gesture drawing, Andrea explains, "Your job is to draw the whole body very quickly." She asks the model to hold ten-second poses. "Just look at the form," she tells them. "Not the details." On her pad she makes bold strokes as the model switches his pose.

"This is what you want," she says, wielding the charcoal with swift lines. "Don't worry if you don't get it. Don't worry if you just put two lines down. Go on to the next."

She holds up her pad, and they all stare doubtfully at the sweeping lines. "What is the point of that?" the boy who wears thick glasses says. Andrea thinks his name is Greg.

"It's to help you see and to free you up," Andrea says. The boy picks up his charcoal and begins to draw. The model, a male student Andrea has seen from time to time in the cafeteria eating macaroni and cheese, is thin but with the well-defined muscles of a dancer. He works well as a model for this life-drawing class. He turns, stretches, reclines. His musculature has good definition, and Andrea admires the thick blue veins that run like rivers down his arms. He is without inhibition.

As her class sketches, Andrea walks around, helping them hold the charcoal, loosening a grip, lightening a stroke. "That's right," she says to the girl with blue hair, "Dawn, that's right . . ."

"Beth."

"Sorry, Beth. It's just a quick upward mark." Andrea makes a swift line on the paper, and Beth blinks. "Don't bother with the details. Look at the tilt of the hips, the tilt of the shoulders. The *contrapposto,* it's called. The twisting of a figure on its axis." Andrea makes a contorted motion with her arms. "Think of Michelangelo's *David.*" She points to the model, who drops his shoulder and turns ever so slightly. The class laughs.

The light streams into the classroom as Andrea moves from student to student. Her reddish-blond hair catches the sun, and one student starts to draw her. Andrea pretends she doesn't notice. She watches the model, the long reach of his arms, his well-defined shape. "Be brave," she says to him, "then be afraid." And to the class, "Try to capture the emotion in each movement." Then she, too, picks up a charcoal and makes bold strokes as the model switches poses.

After class she drives over to the faculty lounge, where high tea is being served. Natalie Winters and Patty Holstern are already waiting for her, as they do most Tuesday afternoons. All three teach on the same day, and this is their standing date, though they don't always make it.

Andrea gives them a wave. She is late, as usual, moving at her frenetic pace. A bag stuffed with papers, books, makeup, and loose change is slung over her shoulder. She hurries to get her tea and finger sandwiches of watercress and smoked salmon. It is a long-term custom at Hartwood to serve high tea in the great Gothic faculty hall on Tuesday and Thursday afternoons (high tea has been endowed by an alum who felt it was an important part of being civilized). Andrea prefers to meet her friends here because the food is free and none of them have to worry about spending money on a meal out.

Natalie and Andrea came to the college the same year. Patty is a newer friend, a professor of art history, who commutes from the city. Beyond their artistic interests, all three share a tenuous relationship to the college. They're hanging on by a thread, as Natalie likes to say. Natalie, a violinist with long white fingers, reclines in a leather armchair, her slender arms and legs draped in odd directions, a cup of tea poised in her lap. She is the one person, besides Charlie, whom Andrea has confided in the most, though lately they haven't spoken much of Andrea's preoccupation, as Natalie calls it, with her father's death.

It was not long after Andrea met Natalie that her father had his accident and it seems as if this accident and subsequent death have defined their entire friendship. Natalie doesn't appear to mind this exactly, though Andrea senses her drifting away. They rarely speak on the phone as they used to and only see each another now at tea. Andrea assumes correctly that Natalie finds her to be "a downer." Andrea finds herself to be "a downer" as well. But Patty remains intrigued by Andrea, as many people are, and by her story—the father who drove off a bridge, the daughter who cared for him in his final illness.

"Patty's going to curate that still-life show at the Brooklyn Museum," Natalie says as Andrea crumples into the leather sofa beside them, her limbs folding up, collapsing into themselves like a card-table.

"Well, that's great, Patty. Congratulations."

"So," Natalie says, "it's been a while."

Andrea thinks back. "Right, I didn't make it last week . . . Where was I?" She looks at her finger sandwiches and realizes she's finding it harder and harder to come here. These sandwiches remind her of Elena's circles, triangles, and squares. At times, lately, all of Hartwood, with its cutbacks and expediency measures and indifference, reminds her of a wicked stepmother in some bad fairy tale.

Natalie shrugs. "Yes, we missed you. But we're here now."

Once a week or so they e-mail to confirm, to see if the others will make it to tea. Otherwise they rarely get together. They intend to have dinner, to meet for lunch, but it doesn't seem to happen. Andrea once looked forward to these meetings in the faculty lounge, to sitting in a leather chair and talking. But lately even this has become a chore.

"Anything new?" Patty asks.

Andrea is never sure how to answer this question. She assumes it is a form of politesse, not a real question. "You know, the usual. Lots to do, student stuff. And trying to get my own work done."

"There aren't enough hours in the day, are there?" Natalie says, stretching her fingers in all directions.

"No, there aren't," Patty says. "And this commute is harder than you can imagine."

"At least you get to be in the city," Natalie whines.

Andrea sits back. Her body is in this room. She is listening to her friends, chattering, well meaning. She knows she can count on them if need be. She could turn to them in a crisis. But she has nothing she wants to say. Nothing she wants to share.

They would, of course, like to know about her love affair with Gil Marken, or why she has not given Charlie, who they think is worth it, another try. But in truth, Andrea's love life doesn't even interest Andrea anymore. It is as if she floats between these two men for friendship and sex, but none of it seems to matter. It mattered once, of course—before she ventured into terrain where no one should ever have to go. But now she scarcely thinks about it at all.

The only thing that matters to her, the only thing she wants to tell anyone, is what no one wants to hear. They want her to talk about biological clocks ticking, about how hard it is to meet men or please their students, about how teaching at Hartwood sucks, or how the autumn has been particularly grueling and nobody has any money or time.

They talk about their careers and their small successes (a chamber orchestra Natalie has been invited to join, Patty's still-life exhibition), and how they are swimming or running or what part of their bodies they like the least (nose for Patty, breasts for Natalie; Andrea would say hips, banging on them).

"Hello, Andrea. Earth to Andrea," Natalie says. It is always like this. As if Andrea is in a dream in some familiar place—a dream whose outcome she knows but can't reach or remember. "We were asking what you think."

Patty and Natalie are poised, expectant. "Where were we?" Andrea asks. Patty smiles, but Natalie seems uneasy as she shifts in her chair.

"Are you okay?" Natalie asks.

What did her father tell her once? You can never die in your own dream. You wake up just before it happens. Unless, of course, you're really dead. Andrea doesn't believe death is part of the journey. She doesn't believe, as with dessert, that the best is being saved for last. The end is the end. But this dream is different. It is taking her somewhere. Inevitably, inexorably, and she cannot stop its trajectory.

"We were talking about the still life," Patty says. "What I like about still life is that it represents the fleeting nature of existence. The objects in the painting are about what is left behind."

Andrea perks up at this. She understands what Patty is saying. Her whole life has been transformed into a still life. Since her father's death everything has been left behind. But they do not know this. And they do not want to know. They don't want to be told about the world she moves through, a foggy landscape in which she is only partially here.

Of course Natalie and Patty, because they are her friends and because they have shared many confidences, know about Andrea's father. They know in gross terms that he had an accident and was in a coma for two years before he died. And they know that he left Andrea and her brother without any money. Which is why they meet over high tea.

But they do not know the rest. That she lives on a dark bridge at night, heading to an unspecified location. That there is a wet and crumpled note in her father's hand, which Andrea keeps trying to read. That she blames her stepmother for sending him out impaired. They do not know that Andrea is stuck in her artwork, painting the same picture over and over again. Or that she is always in two places—the real-time space where the rest of the world dwells, and a bubble, a mental place, that she cannot pop or get out of.

They finish their tea. Natalie has a teacher's meeting, and she rises, her long limbs falling into place as if drawn together by magnets. Patty rises, too. They agree to meet again next week. "Same time," Natalie says.

"Of course," Andrea replies.

As they wander off, Andrea cannot remember a thing they said. As with all the encounters she has been having, this one, too, has evaporated into thin air.

The next day Andrea wakes up feeling groggy. Her head is stuffed up. It is just a cold, but she aches. She has to drag herself out of bed in order to let the dogs out. She microwaves yesterday's coffee, stuffs half a roll of toilet paper into her bag, and heads to the art library, where she spends several hours going through slides. She is sniffling and trying not to touch the images as she prepares a lecture for her life drawing class on the history of the nude.

She tries to focus on the female body. How it disrobed slowly through time. How it went from gossamer to bare. How naked breasts meant something different in the Middle Ages than they did in Victorian times. Her lectures will begin with medieval Madonnas and end with Matisse's *Blue Nude,* the painting that shocked Paris, whose critics called it "reptilian."

Despite her cold, Andrea spends hours looking at slides—breasts nursing the baby Jesus with a nipple daintily exposed, breasts of women slaves with see-through silk draped over them, breasts bared with pride, with snakes crawling across them, with men reaching for them, for all to see. And Matisse's nudes, voluptuous, flaunting.

Andrea thinks of her own breasts. Neat cups that men like to cradle in their hands like coconut shells. Breasts that she has modeled herself. Once a student in a drawing class in the city asked who her plastic surgeon was, and Andrea replied, "God." This was in her braver days. When Andrea thinks of her breasts at all, it is in the context of men sucking on them. In particular, she thinks of Gil Marken, who often shows up at her studio on Wednesday evenings, unless his wife—from whom he was separated when Andrea first met him (though now she isn't so sure)—is in town.

By three in the afternoon she isn't feeling well at all. Her legs hurt, her neck aches, and she wonders if what she has is more serious than a cold. The flu? Meningitis? A sudden onset of rheumatoid arthritis? Andrea is versed in symptoms. She knows them well.

She finds a couch in the reference room and lies down. Closing her eyes, Andrea tries to picture her own body. She can almost see where muscle joins bone. She is sweating, and her heart is beating like a bag of worms, as her father would say. He spoke of the body in poetic terms. A person could turn blue as a robin's egg. A wound would ripen like plums dropping from a tree. Patients were compost—decomposing, biodegradable.

From an early age Andrea has been knowledgeable in the language of disease. She read the books that lined her father's shelves and learned of obscure ailments of the blood, an illness that manifests a rash in the shape of stars, a disorder that makes people walk backward. When she was growing up, she had symptoms of her own. Cluster headaches, sore muscles, dizzy spells, hot hands, cold hands. Digestive ailments. When her father came home from work, she'd report them.

Her symptoms were the one thing that seemed to hold his interest. The more elaborate and complex they were, the more attention he paid. She'd greet him at the door with "I don't know what it is, but when I get up, my legs feel shaky and I have to sit down." Or "My extremities are cold. I seem to bruise so easily."

Her father would take her into his study—that room that smelled of leather and pipe tobacco—where he kept his books of diseases, books he'd hardly opened since medical school, still marked with yellow and red underlining. He would peruse the volumes, trying to match complaint with disease. Though he was not an internist, the diagnoses he did for his daughter appeared to consume him.

When he examined her, Andrea felt his hands, warm and strong, probing. They reached into her spleen, her kidneys, pressing against her appendix, her glands, her thyroid. Sometimes he found small enlargements—a nodule on the thyroid, a cyst under the arm. He lifted her shirt to feel her stomach, check for a swelling in her pelvic area. He never touched her groin or her breasts. If her complaint centered on those areas, he told her to speak with her mother.

Andrea was not sure when she started to exaggerate her symptoms. She wanted to see how clever he was, what elaborate diagnosis he'd come up with. Whether, at last, he'd call her a fake. She didn't invent them, exactly, but she made them more interesting than they might have been otherwise. If she got up suddenly and felt dizzy, she'd tell him that the world had taken a spin. If she had a less than perfect bowel movement, she'd describe her digestive distress. Once he heard something in her chest, a flutter, as if she were taking flight. "What're you running from?" he asked. "Are you afraid?"

She shook her head. Still, her heart beat as if someone was trying to escape. In China, he told her, they eat a small quail-like bird. It is so fragile that you just have to press your thumb to its chest, and it keels over, dead.

When she opens her eyes, it is dark out. Andrea feels feverish. For a moment she doesn't know where she is. Then she remembers. She's in the library. Her head feels heavy, as if it has been weighted down with stones. Like a body, underwater. She has no time for illness. But she thinks she should head home. Open a can of soup.

As she packs up her books and is leaving the library, she passes a cubicle where a woman is hunched over, staring into space. The woman has several books open in front of her. Her glasses lie beside the books, and she seems to be in a daze.

It takes Andrea a few moments to realize that the woman is Loretta. At first Andrea mistakes her for a kind of portrait, like a Vermeer, of a woman caught in a pause. Loretta is surrounded by large tomes—books on psychology and social pathology. Andrea hesitates, then decides to say hello. She takes a step toward her, and Loretta turns and stares. She stares at Andrea with glassy eyes, as if she has never seen her before. Then Andrea realizes she doesn't see her at all. "Loretta, it's Andrea."

"Oh, God, Andrea." Loretta laughs, pushing her books to the side. "I don't even know where I am."

"I'm sorry. I shouldn't have interrupted you."

"Oh, this is how I work. I get completely lost."

Andrea feels the weight of her own books on her hip. "I can understand that."

"Sometimes I don't even know where I am." Loretta rubs her eyes, looking tired. "I don't often come here. The lights aren't very kind, are they?"

Andrea laughs. "No, they aren't."

Loretta scrutinizes Andrea more carefully. "You don't look well. Are you all right?"

"I don't know. I think I'm a little feverish."

Loretta raises her hand, and instinctively Andrea stoops down. Loretta's cold palm touches her forehead. "You are feverish," she says. "You should get home."

Andrea nods, feeling somehow relieved. It's not just in her head. She really is sick. "Yes, I'd better get going. I don't want you to get what I have. Anyway, I didn't want to interrupt you. I just wanted to tell you I appreciated your note."

"Call me when you're feeling better," Loretta says, waving a hand as if there is nothing to apologize for. "We must get together. For dinner or something. Maybe I'll have the Vitales as well. Soon."

"Yes." Andrea smiles. Her skin feels prickly, hot, but cooler where Loretta placed her hand. "Yes, I'd like that."

For two days she is sick, moving in and out of a semidelirious state. Mrs. Romanelli brings up some soup and checks on her from time to time. Her mother calls, offering to stop by, but Andrea tells her not to bother and goes back to sleep for another day. When Andrea wakes up, she sees Charlie standing by her bed. "How'd you get here?" she asks.

"You called me, remember?"

She shakes her head. "No, I don't. Am I that sick?"

"You seemed pretty out of it." He's straightening the covers, picking up dirty Kleenex off the floor. "Anyway, the door was open." He puts a hand on her forehead. "Have you seen a doctor?"

Andrea shakes her head. "It's just a cold. Maybe the flu."

He's brought a bagful of over-the-counter medicine. He makes her take some aspirin and drink a glass of ice water. "Andrea, I'm worried about you. You don't seem to be taking care of yourself." He looks in her fridge. All he finds is a container of yogurt and a bottle of Scotch. "This isn't going to make you well."

"It's practically full," she says.

Charlie shrugs. "You need food. You look terrible."

"Well, I'm sick," she tells him.

He settles down on the couch and reads a magazine. Andrea watches him as she slips feverishly in and out of sleep. It is so comfortable, so easy, having him here. A portrait of domesticity. If only it could be like this. She doesn't like to think that before Charlie, there were others. Many others. Too many to count.

Most were one-night stands, weekend flings. There were men she met on trips to Jamaica and others who lived upstate, in a bungalow colony in the Catskills, in Chicago, on another coast, or, once, another continent. She did long-distance well and specialized in men who weren't really around. One or two had drug problems. One gave her a black eye.

What she liked about Charlie was the possibility of normal life.

"I want a man who calls me when he says he will and actually shows up," she told her brother.

"Good luck," he'd replied. But soon she felt restless. The normal life became too predictable. A man should not remind her of a clock. She wanted surprises. Zebras, kumquats, tickets to Belize. Now she sees Charlie, sitting on her couch, dozing, and thinks this is what it would be like to be together. She tries to decide if this is a good or a bad thing. She wonders how long it would be before she grew restless again.

Charlie stays with her much of the afternoon, bringing her tea with ginger and heating up the soup Mrs. Romanelli brought the other day. He walks the dogs and rinses the dishes in the sink. She sees him on the couch, reading or watching TV, as she drifts in and out of sleep. At dusk she hears him head out again with the dogs. Then the dogs come back alone and curl up on her bed. She hears his car pull away, then she sleeps until the next afternoon.

On Friday she wakes up late, her fever broken. She's feeling better. She gets up, walks the dogs. She remembers to call Charlie and leave a message that says "Thanks." She wants to say more. She wishes she could, but she's not sure what more would be. So it's just "You were nice to me, as always . . . I owe you now."

She decides she's well enough to head back to the library. She works there for an hour or so, bent over slides of the bodies of women. When she takes a break, she checks the cubicles to see if Loretta is working again today. In her head she rehearses how she will say it to her: "I'm feeling better. Thought I'd take you up on your offer." But Loretta is nowhere to be found.

In the early evening Andrea realizes she is famished. It occurs to her that she has barely eaten in days. She goes to a diner off campus that caters to students, a good, cheap place. She eats meat loaf, mashed potatoes, creamed spinach, drinks a glass of wine. Then she takes the long drive to her studio.

The studio is located at the far end of the campus, in the Rinkley Visual Arts Center, a stark limestone building. It was donated by a well-known alum, a lover of the arts. It is already dark as she pulls into the parking lot. As she gets out of her car, she looks behind her, wary of being followed. Not that she has been followed before, but there have been reports of heinous crimes. Young women abducted, horrific Internet encounters gone awry.

And then there are the "bad" neighborhoods of Hartwood, in the warehouses near the river, where there are said to be gangs that rob or maim for sport. Sometimes these gangs drift into the college neighborhoods, despite the security patrols, the college's efforts to keep its students and faculty safe. There have been some racial incidents and one case of gay bashing, a young man beaten senseless with a lead pipe.

Andrea cannot rid herself of these thoughts as she makes her way up the asphalt walk toward the darkened building. There are only five or six other art teachers in the school who use the building, but no one seems to come here as often as Andrea. As she walks to the entryway, key in hand, Andrea tries to remember if these dark thoughts of being followed, of men with lead pipes and worse, haunted her before her father's accident. Even as she turns the key she can't seem to let go of the way her father died. She wonders what he went through. What was he thinking as he drove?

She sees him in the car with the radio on. A classical station. It is a Friday evening. Perhaps a Beethoven symphony. Live from Symphony Hall. He would be humming. Following the strings, then the horns. Conducting with only one hand on the wheel.

Then she blanks out. She cannot imagine past this moment. Her father fighting sleep, trying to stay awake, his eyelids closing. He knows the bridge is coming. That bridge. The one over Thompkin's Creek. It was a turn that always came up fast. As a teenager, Andrea took it many times, alone or with some boy. Often they had been drinking, and suddenly it was upon you.

But no one had ever missed the curve before. It had never happened, not even to some teenager out cruising or in search of a secluded place. Surely it should not have happened to Simon Geller. He'd have no doubt of what lay ahead. The curve, then the bridge, for which he'll have to slow down. But he does not. He feels his eyes closing as he grows drowsy. Thoughts of sleep overcome him. His foot is on the gas as he flies like a bird.

Andrea is trembling as the elevator doors close. No one leaps to attack her inside, though her heart pounds in her chest as if someone has. The creaky elevator carries her, one jolting floor at a time, to the fifth floor. She walks along the dank corridor to her studio, where she flicks on the switch.

The room is suddenly illuminated with harsh fluorescent light. Taped to a worktable is a faded Xerox of a picture. It is a copy of the photograph of the house her father built on Shallow Lake—the picture Elena sent her, the one that hangs in her entryway across from her bed. On the floor and on the walls are nearly forty canvases of this same plot of land, the white house with the wraparound porch.

This is what she paints. It is her only subject now. She paints on canvas and wood, paper and cardboard—wide panoramic, the house, the lake, the farmland around it. She uses different techniques, burning the wood to make the house look as if it is on fire. She has purchased aging topographical maps and painted the house in perfect representation on them.

She etches and carves and sculpts. She makes layered collages out of cut paper, the way children do. She creates the house in all seasons, in disrepair and ruin, in recollected splendor, from a myriad of angles. She breaks its windows, opens its doors. Glues photos and newspaper headlines across its facade. Hacks its walls, hurls rag dolls with torn-out arms on its lawn. Roadkill in the driveway. She makes it a childhood memory; she makes it the scene of a crime.

Shallow Lake wasn't really that shallow. In fact, it was deep. Her father always warned them about it. He said, "Looks are deceiving." No one knew why it was named Shallow Lake. Her father thought it was because the people who first went there never walked out very far. Once you ventured a hundred yards or more, the lake dropped off.

The danger of the lake was its center. No one was sure where the bottom was. The stories of its tragedies and secrets were legend. Once, before the Gellers bought land there, a boy was said to have fallen off a boat in the middle of the lake. He was wearing his school backpack, and the weight of it pulled him down. They dredged the lake for weeks but weren't able to reach bottom, and the boy was never found. Robby never believed this story. It sounded to him like a warning to parents and their children, but Andrea believed it, and it terrified her that a boy lay in the middle of the lake with his backpack still strapped on.

Andrea tried to picture what was inside that backpack. She envisioned the boy stuck eternally in fifth grade, with heavy textbooks of American history, biology, math, perhaps the paperback of *The Red Badge of Courage*. Fruit Loops, a pencil case, stickers, number 2 pencils, a slide rule, a Marvel comic book, a plastic giveaway toy from Burger King.

It was difficult for Andrea to be out on the lake and not think about the boy. She imagined more objects in the backpack than it could have possibly contained. In art school she did an installation. She painted dozens of tiny pictures of the lake, a small boat, the boy. Then she assembled all the things she envisioned in his backpack over the years.

She brought together all the tangible objects and then the intangible—the memories, the grudges, childhood pleasures and disappointments—he carried. She included a bicycle he'd dreamed of, a girl he'd liked, a superhero he'd imagined himself to be. Her first installation, entitled *Backpack,* filled an entire room and spilled out into the hall.

Though they were raised in Montrose, outside of Poughkeepsie, the children called Shallow Lake home. Their father had bought property in the Adirondacks not long after he and Barbara married. He had designed the house himself—a long white building with its wraparound porch, a big open kitchen, sleeping alcoves, picture windows. Over summers and vacations he had helped the builders construct it.

In the divorce it was the one thing he had refused to give up. He had given Barbara everything—the house in Montrose, the car, a chunk of his salary. But he would not give her Shallow Lake. It was where he planned to retire. It was where he expected his grandchildren to spend their summers.

Andrea loved the lake as well. The calls of the loons, the mist rising in the morning; in winter, skating on its glassy surface. It was on Shallow Lake that she'd first seen the dragonflies. They bred along the shore and skimmed the waters. Their shades of blue and green caught her eye. There were millions. The dragonflies, her father explained, ate the gnats.

He used to take her fishing. She did not like to fish, but because he liked it, she went along. She did not like to put the bait on the hook or to pull the hook out of the fish's mouth. She could not look at a creature with a hook in its mouth, lips ripped in two. "It's just a fish," her father explained, "it doesn't have our neurological system. It doesn't feel pain . . ." adding, almost as an afterthought, "like we do."

But as the fish struggled, twisting, she had difficulty believing him. It seemed obvious that the fish felt pain. As her father dangled it from the hook, its eyes bulged, looking straight at her.

Andrea switches off the overhead light and turns on an amber floor lamp she prefers when she is setting up. She slips out of her clothes into the baggy pants and flannel shirt she wears when painting. Then she walks around the room, surveying her work, adjusting a picture or two.

She has just completed #37 in this series and tonight she will begin work on #38. Andrea had envisioned a series of fifty paintings, but now she knows it will be more. Not because she isn't ready for it to be done, but because she cannot think of anything she will paint beyond this series.

She is not sure what #38 will be, but then she never is. She anticipates some kind of spectral light, a woman—perhaps divested of her limbs—on the porch. Andrea allows the painting to guide her, to take on a life of its own. She has no interest in consciousness or ideas. She never knows before or even after what she has done. Her work comes to her in a kind of trance, and she is always surprised when she is finished.

She has just set up a canvas, laid out the paints, when her cell phone rings. She looks at the number and knows it is Gil and that he wants to come over. One of the places they like to meet is in her studio, after hours. He can easily make an excuse to Lila that he is working late at the library. Besides, Lila is often at literary events in the city. It is not that difficult for Andrea and Gil to have their affair.

But tonight she is not sure she wants to see him. "Couldn't you have called me earlier?" she says into the phone. Until a few minutes ago she was hoping he would call. All week she anticipated it. But now she feels a painting starting to rise within her, and she fears it will go away. Still, he is a man she's had trouble saying no to. When she is not with Gil, she thinks of him. Not in his entirety but in his parts. The parts in this case being greater than the whole. His hand on the curve of her spine. His lips on her neck, her breasts. Normally just the thought of him is enough to arouse her.

Though she finds him stiff in social settings, he is not that way when he is alone with her. The first time they were together, after a party, when he offered to drive her home but instead detoured to a wooded area, she was surprised. There is something about the way he makes love to her—the way he seems to know her body—that excites her. She thinks he is the kind of man who, if she would let him, would use restraining devices. Sex toys. Velcro straps. She has envisioned herself tied to the bed—a cameo role in a Loretta Partlow novel.

"I wasn't sure if Lila was going into town until a little while ago," he says.

Andrea shrugs. It is one of the annoyances in this recent phase of their relationship. Since Lila returned home. She can never call him. He has to call her. There is no telling when he'll be driving with Lila to IKEA or a lecture at school. Andrea doesn't like this waiting time. She doesn't want to see him tonight, not really. She wants to do her work, but she knows she will see him.

It has been difficult to extricate herself. When they met at a faculty meeting, he said his marriage was over and that Lila was living in a studio apartment in New York. Which was true at the time. It was common knowledge in Hartwood that Lila Marken had moved to the city. Andrea and Gil were friends for weeks, having coffee and then dinners, before anything happened between them. He charmed his way into her life with his attentions, his capacity for listening, his seeming interest in everything she did.

They became lovers. Slowly, tentatively. Gil embedded his way into her life. Just as slowly, Andrea noted Lila's return. She came home for parties, for events. "It means nothing," Gil assured Andrea. But Lila began staying over. Soon Gil couldn't meet Andrea on weekends because Lila was in town. And then, just as Andrea found herself involved with this man, his wife moved home. Andrea had tried to pull away. Every few weeks she'd refuse Gil's calls. She would tell herself that his excuses were lies. But it was not so easy.

She still looks forward to drinking wine with Gil and making love. Those weeks when he doesn't call, when he can't get away, she is disappointed. She is left with a hollow feeling she can never quite name, as if life is pointless and nothing matters. But tonight his visit feels like an interruption.

In the half hour it takes him to arrive, Andrea isn't sure what to do with herself. She doesn't have enough time to start painting. She doesn't like this waiting. To work she needs long stretches in which she can lose herself. She's not the kind of painter who can grab a few moments here or there. Still, when she thinks of Gil, it is, in a way, this waiting that makes her want him more. It is a peculiar kind of desire over which she has little control. But in the time it takes him to drive over she prepares her paints. Sets up her canvas. She intends to begin work on *The House on Shallow Lake #38* after he is gone.

She has some ideas coalescing when he calls again to say he is there. Grumbling, she goes downstairs to let him in. They do not touch until they are in the elevator, its doors closed, in case someone is watching, wondering what a tenured professor in the math department is doing over at Rinkley. Then he pulls her to him. His hands are everywhere—her backside, her breasts.

"I've missed you," he groans, gripping her against him. He doesn't let go of her until they are out of the elevator and inside her studio. He has brought a bottle of red wine, which he uncorks and pours into two glasses. He takes a sip, declares it drinkable. Then they slump onto the couch and sip together as he gazes around her studio. "I see you've got some new work." He raises his chin, his blue eyes looking around the room. "I like it a lot."

"What do you like about it?" Andrea tries to remember how long it has been since he was here. A week or two? More?

"It's so . . . obsessive."

"Is it?" she asks. "Actually, I think I'm in a rut." She gets up, starts walking around. Talking about her work makes her nervous. Having him come here and see it does, too. She goes to the window, staring out.

"Doesn't seem like you're in a rut to me." He walks over to where she is, reaches for her from behind. He runs his hands over her breasts, down her thighs. He cups his hand between her legs. Instinctively she thinks of Charlie, wishing he could be unpredictable in this way. She wishes she could take these two men and roll them into one.

Without her turning around, they take off their clothes. His hands stay between her legs, and Andrea remains pressed against the window, wondering if anyone can see her naked body, contorting, pressed to the glass. She is aroused by the thought that someone can.

With his fingers he opens her. His hands slip to her buttocks and back up to her breasts, squeezing her nipples. He makes love to her from behind, never looking at her. He turns her around only when they are done.

Afterward, they stretch out on her couch, sipping his wine. She curls against him, her hand resting on his thigh. She closes her eyes; then the old thoughts, her agitation, returns. After a few moments she sits up. "Can I ask you something?"

Gil sighs, stroking her hair. "I have a feeling I don't—"

"I've been thinking about my stepmother and what she did."

"I know you have." Gil rolls slightly away. His family came from Sweden, and he is a pale, hulking man. He has made it clear that he wants this affair to be easy, a break from the routine of his marriage. Not one more thing he has to deal with. He has little patience for protracted emotional scenes, and it seems as if he has been losing patience with Andrea for several months now.

Gil Marken has one small claim to fame. It has to do with a problem called the philosopher's chopstick, which Andrea doesn't quite understand. If ten philosophers are having Chinese food and each one has only one chopstick, how long, if they share, will it take for them to eat their meal? Or something like that. All Andrea knows is that Gil's solution to this problem was a major contribution to shortcut theory. Which led to browsers.

Expediency is what Gil wants from a love affair as well.

"Just listen once more."

Gil nods, his arms raised above his head.

"I've been thinking about this for a long time. Elena turned him against us. She wanted him out of the way. I'm sure she overmedicated him, but I can't prove it. She let him go out that night—"

"I know." Gil sighs.

Andrea shifts on the couch, rising up on her elbows. "You know Loretta better than I do. I want to get her to write the story of what happened to my father." He sits up. He seems sleepy but slightly more interested. "My stepmother is a big reader and a fan of Loretta's work. I want Elena to read it. I want her to know that even if I can't do anything to her, I know."

"Oh." Gil smiles, cocking his head. "Like Hamlet."

Andrea nods. "Yes, I suppose." She hadn't quite seen it this way herself, but now she does. The play within the play. She sits up, tucking her legs under her. She reaches for Gil's shirt and slips it over her shoulders. "I've begun to run into Loretta. She's had me over for drinks. She keeps asking, and I'm ready to tell her what happened to him. But how do I get her to do this? Do I say, 'Here's my story; I want you to write it'?"

Gil shakes his head. "No, she wouldn't like that."

"I didn't think she would. So how do I do it?"

"She'd have to feel as if she came to it on her own." Gil hesitates, then wraps his arm around Andrea, pulling her close. "Tell her your story in confidence."

At this Andrea smiles. "You mean as if it's a secret?"

"Yes," he says. "Tell her she can't tell a soul."

Three

"My garden is an extension of myself," Loretta writes in *Snippets and Cuttings*. Andrea looks down at Loretta's fall garden with the book open in her lap. She tries to determine just what that means as she gazes from the garden to the passage she has highlighted in yellow.

Beyond her renown as a novelist, Loretta is known for her garden. She has called it her great hobby, her true avocation. "If I had not been captivated by words, I would have been captivated by plants," she writes. For many years Loretta has written "The Gardener's Euonymus" in a local newspaper, under the pseudonym Marilyn Bloom. All the columns had puns as titles, such as "Held Hosta" and "The Beet Goes On." But she also wrote quite seriously on how to achieve continuous bloom, what to do with a shady corner, the soil chemistry for blue hydrangeas.

Photographers from all over the world who have come to photograph the novelist often do so in her garden. It has been featured in *Garden Design, Home Gardens,* and *Celebrity Homes.* Her organic vegetable and herb patch has won prizes. Many of Loretta's book photos show her in the garden. As she once wrote, "Isak Dinesen said, 'I like to cook and sometimes write.' Jack London considered himself a rancher. I am a gardener who writes in the off-season."

Andrea has come to appreciate the gift of this garden. It is one of the few things, since her father's accident, that has brought her any peace. *Snippets and Cuttings* is a book Andrea has read several times. She has dog-eared pages, marked passages she likes: "A garden is one long revision—an endless edit. This is a writer's work as well."

As Andrea looks down, she admires the tall leafy grasses that drape into flowering shrubs, the variegated hosta leaves that brighten the dark walkways beside the house. She tries to understand how Loretta fills it in with so much color and how she knows what to plant next to what.

Soon Loretta appears, dragging a large bag of cedar mulch. As she bends with a shovel, scooping out the mulch, Andrea tugs on her jeans and red flannel shirt. She puts on a gray parka and heads down. She leaves the dogs at home, though they bark as she pretends to be making her way toward the walk in the woods.

She passes Loretta's house and gives a wave. "Hi there," she shouts. "I see you're working. The mums look beautiful."

"You think so." Loretta says thoughtfully. "They seem to be fading already. And we just put them in."

"Oh, no, I think they are lovely."

Loretta steps back to get a better view. "I wish there was something blue besides the salvia. We've tried Russian sage, but the soil isn't sandy enough and we don't get enough sun."

Andrea looks at the salvia. "Maybe you should stake it."

"Oh, you know your plants." Loretta gives the salvia a critical gaze. "Yes, I probably should."

Andrea pauses in the walkway. "I love looking at your garden," she says. "I'd like to paint it sometime."

Loretta shrugs, then smiles. "Anytime."

"Well, usually I take pictures. I keep them. I always paint from photographs."

"That would be fine. Many people have photographed this garden." Loretta rubs her lower back. "Would you like to have some tea?"

"No, I want to be outside," Andrea says. "Could I help you? Would you like a hand?"

Loretta looks at her oddly, then says, "I don't usually have people help me. This garden is really an extension of my work."

"I know," Andrea says. "You wrote that."

"Did I?"

"Yes, in *Snippets and Cuttings*, you wrote, 'My garden is an extension of myself.' It's almost the same thing, isn't it?"

"Yes, I suppose. Almost. If you assume that I am my work."

"Well," Andrea says, "aren't you?"

Loretta cocks her head. "Yes. I suppose I am." She gives Andrea a quizzical look. "I had no idea you had read me so carefully."

"Oh," Andrea says with a laugh, "I suppose I have. Now," she holds out her hands, "show me what to do."

Loretta bends and digs into the bag. She takes a handful of red mulch and spreads it at the base of the plants, then smooths it out. Andrea pulls out a handful as well. She is surprised by the loamy wetness, the rich cedary smell. On her knees, she cups the mulch and puts it around the plants. She spreads it along the ground, then digs back in the bag for more.

It is such a simple gesture, but it makes Andrea want to cry. Perhaps because it is so simple. This is what life should be like, she thinks, digging into a bag, letting your hands smooth the chips at the base of fall plants.

They work side by side in silence for half an hour. Then Andrea says, "I'm going for my walk now."

"Well, thank you," Loretta says, her face red from exertion. "It was nice having you here."

Andrea heads off into the woods. She walks slowly, wishing she'd brought her dogs. It is another beautiful day, and she whistles to herself as she goes.

Andrea arranges the room into a kind of musical-chairs format. There are two rows, facing each other, about six feet apart. In front of half of them, she has set up easels and drawing pads, with pencil and charcoal. Her students file in, uncertain of what to do. "Just take a chair," Andrea says. "Wherever you like."

She makes a mental note of which students gravitate to the easels and which to the chairs with no drawing materials in front of them. She is not surprised by how they divide themselves. Beth and Marc, her most talented students, immediately go to the easels. Greg, the boy who questions her every time, sits across.

When all fifteen are present, Andrea says, "Today we are doing portraits of one another, but we will be doing them as a rotation." She points to the students with the easels in front of them. "You will begin to draw the person sitting across from you. I will keep time, and every few minutes I will ask you to shift chairs, so that each of you will be working on each portrait. Then we will switch and the models will draw."

Beth smiles, and Andrea sees that she understands, but Greg, who slumps in his chair, does not. "What's the point of this?" he asks.

"The point is I want you to learn from one another. I want you to see the mistakes and strengths of your fellow students. And . . ." She hesitates as she thinks this through. "I don't want you to hold on to your art. I don't want you to feel as if your precious strokes belong to you."

"I don't understand."

"It's about the process. It's not about you." They all look at her and nod. Then they settle into their seats and begin.

After class, as Andrea is racing between appointments and a meeting with her chairperson, then having to rush back to see a student and maybe grab some lunch, she runs into Loretta. In fact, she almost literally runs into her. Loretta has to grab Andrea by the arms. "Oh, Andrea," Loretta says with a laugh. "You're like the Mad Hatter."

Andrea pauses. Loretta is perhaps the only person she would stop for. Loretta, dressed in a long red coat with dark glasses that seem more appropriate for Paris than Hartwood, tries to make small talk. "How are you? Do you have time for lunch?"

"I am so sorry, but I have a meeting." Andrea glances at her watch, then frowns. "Yikes," she says. "Already late."

"You always seem to be in a hurry, Andrea," Loretta says. "You need to slow down. Give yourself more time between things. Do some belly breathing, you know, like in yoga."

Andrea nods. "You're right. I should do that." She takes a deep breath, lets it out with a heavy sigh.

"I like your jacket." Loretta touches the lapel. It is brightly colored, embroidered. "You know, if you cram too much in, life will pass you by."

Ignoring the last comment, Andrea says, "It's from India or Tibet. I haven't been, but I got it in the East Village."

"Well, you'll have to take me sometime," Loretta says, fondling the sleeve. "To the East Village, that is."

"Yes, I will," Andrea says. Promising to call soon, she rushes away. In truth, she is often late—to class, to her office hours. Sometimes she misses appointments. But more than that, she always has a sense of being rushed, a breathless feeling that she must be at the next place, though she doesn't know for certain where that place is. People have called her abrupt, but really it is that she is so often scattered, running behind, squeezing things in at the last moment.

Charlie used to comment on this. When he would shape his hands into "time out" (a gesture she defined as pedestrian), he meant it. "You need to take a break," he'd tell her over and over again. But Andrea never takes a break. She doesn't know what to do with empty space, empty time, except clutter it, fill it up like a kitchen drawer when company is expected. She always has a million things to do, places to be. A walk, a class, something she must buy. No time to sit still.

Except in her studio. Often it takes her a long while to get there—she has to pick up coffee and walk the dogs, she has to make sure her e-mail is answered and her schoolwork is ready—but once she is inside, something drops away. Here it is as if Andrea has stepped out of her scattered self. A new person emerges—focused, on task, clear. She doesn't have a clock except on her cell phone, which is usually off. There is a radio that she can turn on if she wants, but she rarely does. She wants silence, no distractions. She paints at night until she's too tired to go on. First she stretches her canvas or selects a piece of wood, if she is working in wood. She picks her materials. She works for hours, until her arm aches and she can barely lift the brush.

That night as she paints with the bright lights on, she has no idea what time it is or how long she has been here. She does not even hear the man open her door and peer in. She does not know he is there until he says hello. Then she shrieks. "Oh my God," she shouts, clutching at her heart.

Garcia, the security guard, is standing there in his blue uniform, walkie-talkie in his hand. "I'm sorry, miss," he says, "I just wanted to know—I wanted to be sure you were all right." He's just doing his job, Andrea tells herself, but she is annoyed. Doesn't he know these are artists' studios? That people might be working into the night?

She presses her hand to her heart as if she could slow it down. "You startled me."

"Well, it just seemed awful late for someone to be up here."

"Look, it's my studio. This is when I work."

He takes off his cap, runs his hand through his wavy hair. "Hey, it's like you're living here. You need a life."

Now she is furious. Where'd they get this guy? Rent-a-Cop? She wants to yell at him. Instead she speaks firmly, slowly, so that she is understood. "This is my life. And I'd prefer you not intrude on it."

After that night his visits are sporadic. "I could be bludgeoned to death, and it would take days for anyone to find me," she tells Robby. Her brother, who works for a sporting magazine in San Francisco, has also told her to get a life. And he has told her to stop obsessing about whatever happened with their father.

He sends her little quotes, her horoscopes, thoughts for the day: "You are trapped within the prison of yourself." A few months ago he mailed her a clipping about a racehorse named Zippy Chippy. Zippy Chippy has lost all ninety-three of his races because he looks at the other horses when he comes out of the gate. "This is called dwelling," the article said. Robby had underlined the word in red three times. "It is a fatal flaw in racehorses."

"You have to move on," he tells her when she tries to talk to him.

"Security guards, brothers, old boyfriends, I don't need all these people telling me what to do," Andrea retorts. "I am moving on. You just don't see."

When she is not at her studio, Andrea stays up, rereading the novels of Loretta Partlow. She believes that if she keeps reading this work, she will find a clue to her own life. She thinks some secret is encoded here. That she and the novelist have been thrown together for a reason. Not just for Andrea's plan to get back at Elena, but for something even more. Something neither of them can know. Andrea never believed in destiny before, but now she does.

These nights Loretta's studio is often illumined as well. Andrea can see her hunched over her desk, a shadow crossing the room. This was not always the case. For years, when Andrea could not sleep and would gaze down, she saw only blackness. Now there is this one light, burning, an amber spot of hope.

Andrea sits rereading the prologue to *What If?*. It is perhaps the story that has stayed with her the most—a heart-wrenching narrative of a boy whose older brother is kidnapped on their way to school. The kidnapper tells the nine-year-old that he will kill his older brother if he goes home and tells. So for hours the younger boy dallies in the woods. The novel is told from the point of view of the younger brother, looking back from years later at his life.

The novel was written with such poignancy and detail that some critics sensed an autobiographical piece: something that had happened in Loretta Partlow's life that no one knew about. It is her most tender, most carefully written work. Now Andrea wonders if the clue she has been searching for is hidden in here:

This is the difficult part. The part I have been unable to explain, not to my parents or the police, and certainly not to myself. What was I doing in the woods those two hours instead of racing home? Why didn't I run straight to my house? And what if I had? What if I hadn't obeyed the man who took my brother away? What if I'd gone right away and told?

Would they have found my brother?

Would they have captured the man?

And would my life have been different from the one I am living?

I cannot bear thinking of the unspeakable things that have been done to my brother. But in their own way, unspeakable things have been done to me.

But what if I had not listened to the man? If I had run home screaming as loudly as I could?

Then perhaps my life would not have become this series of questions and doubts, pauses and speculations, about what might have been.

It is a warm day of Indian summer—the air smelling of rotting leaves, of decomposition—when Andrea runs into Loretta, her hair pulled back. She's at the entrance to the trail and wearing a fisherman's sweater, red scarf, and jeans. Their dogs growl at one another at first, then do their circular dance. Andrea is surprised to see her since it is after eight, and normally Loretta would have been out for her walk earlier.

"This is late for you, isn't it?" Andrea says.

"Yes, I don't know why. I didn't get up. Even Patrick slept in. He has a meeting, so I decided to come out alone." She touches Andrea lightly on the arm. "I always need to start my day with a walk. Shall we go together? That is, if I can keep up with you. Or perhaps you'd prefer to go alone?"

"I always go around the pond, then under the bridge near the culvert. There's a nice walk there."

"Show me your way."

Andrea heads off to the right and Loretta follows. The dogs race ahead, sniffing, then come back to their owners. The path is soft underfoot, a bed of pine needles, fallen leaves, mulch. The ground is dry and it is easy to walk. They walk briskly, laughing at how Kippy and Pablo seem to like each other. "They're about the same size," Andrea says.

They make a circular loop toward the pond, which is sizable—

about half a mile around. A family of ducks paddles by. Andrea spots a blue heron on the other side and they stop to look at it. "They migrate this time of year," Loretta says. "I often see them in the fall."

"Yes, I do, too. This is a big migratory path for aquatic birds," Andrea tells her. Loretta smiles, nodding. They begin walking again, continuing their path around the pond. Across the pond the heron stretches its wings. There is a loud flap.

"I've been thinking about you," Loretta says, her voice growing quiet, almost a whisper. "It's so odd how you can live so near someone and never know much about them. Not have a clue about what's happening in their lives."

Andrea nods. "Yes, it's true. I hardly know the truth about anyone around me. Starting with myself." She laughs at her own joke, and Loretta laughs with her.

Andrea anticipates the next comment. That Loretta wants to know more. It is what Andrea has waited for and what she has dreaded, because she knows it will take her to a place from which she cannot come back.

"You know, Jim Adler has said such interesting things about your new paintings," Loretta says.

"Oh really, he has?"

"Yes. And so has Gil Marken. I didn't appreciate that you two were friends. He's a fascinating man. Difficult to be close to, I imagine, but interesting. One of those men who is probably worth the trouble."

Andrea frowns, feeling embarrassed at the mention of Gil. "I met him at a faculty meeting a year ago. I guess he was separated then." She wonders if Loretta is fishing, hoping to find out more, but she doesn't mention him again.

"Well, Jim is a big admirer of yours. You seem to know so much about my work, and I don't know much about yours, though I admired *Dragonfly* . . ."

"That was a long time ago." Andrea laughs. "Anyway, I can walk into a store and just buy yours."

Loretta nods. "That's true. I don't know if this would be inconvenient or inappropriate, but I'd love to visit your studio sometime and see what you're working on."

Andrea is taken aback. To see her work. She is both flattered and surprised. Though she has been a practicing artist for two decades, she is hardly a household name. There were those few early successes, but it has been a while since she's had a major show. She has been in several group shows, including one in Seattle, and one local show that Jim Adler helped curate. Recently she had an installation in a Chelsea gallery—a piece called *Window Pain*, which consisted of cartoon-like images and text made up of typos. But critics called this work "trivial" compared to what had come before.

She had expected the busy novelist to want to know more about her private grief, but she had not anticipated that Loretta would want to see her paintings. In fact, Loretta seems less interested in her personal life than Andrea would have imagined. Andrea is pleased by this interest in her as an artist. She hardly ever shows her work-in-progress. But she says yes. "Just give me a call whenever you'd like to come by."

They pause to watch a pair of wild swans circling the pond, the male with his wings unfurled, in quiet pursuit of his mate. The three dogs race to the pond, barking, but the swans, knowing they are at a safe distance, pay them no heed.

On Saturday morning Loretta phones to ask, "Would this weekend be convenient to visit your studio?" Andrea is flustered. She had not anticipated this call so soon. She thought Loretta might get busy and forget. Or that she was just being polite. But they make a plan to drive over to the studio on Sunday.

Andrea goes over that afternoon to straighten up, uncover paintings she wants on display. She finds she is dismayed by the prospect of this studio visit, suddenly embarrassed by the run-down room she paints in, the sagging couch with its unmentionable stains where she and her married lover lie. She tosses a bedspread over it.

And the work, which she has been enjoying, now looks unrealized. She wishes her technique were better and that she had more to say. The sameness of the images disturbs her. Though she knows she's not the best judge of her own work, the paintings do not seem as distinctive as they have in her other series. In this regard her brother might be right. She is not ready to move on. She wishes she could paint something different. Or go deeper with what she has. But she seems stuck on this one thing.

She is reminded of a friend from art school, a girl whose mother was paralyzed with a crippling disease and could move only her head. All the girl did was make hundreds of lifelike plaster-of-paris images of her mother's head. It was a strange compulsion, but the girl admitted that she had no interest in anything other than the heads. Years later, Andrea saw a show of this girl's work in a SoHo gallery and found a cumulative effect to the repetition. The girl went on to develop a minor career with these heads.

But Andrea isn't sure yet what she is accomplishing with her *House on Shallow Lake* series. She has dozens of these images in every season, in every state of disrepair, with hovering shadows and torn-apart dolls, with people sitting on the porch eating, unaware of a darkness coming over them from the side of a painting. Encircled in barbed wire. Limbs growing like weeds from the lawn. She has tried to paint other things—a portrait of Charlie, naked and splayed on the couch; another of a faceless Gil; landscapes; a still life at her home. But in the end she could not lose herself in them. They were exercises, not pieces of her heart. A goal for Andrea when she paints is to forget where she is. She wants to be in the place she is painting from, and with these paintings she never was.

She cleans her studio, but not too much, because she does not want Loretta to think she came here to get ready for the visit. There is order in her disorder. She displays against the wall, hanging on the wall, the work she is most proud of. She stays late, trying to paint, but feels too distracted. Instead she goes home and drinks half a bottle of wine and falls asleep.

Because Loretta plans to stay on campus and work at the library, they have decided to caravan. Loretta drives cautiously, at a snail's pace behind Andrea. Andrea keeps an eye on her in the rearview mirror. More than once she has to pull over because Loretta has missed a light or a turn. A red car cuts in between them, and Andrea sees Loretta become disoriented, so she pulls over again.

She can barely see Loretta peering over the wheel. It is as if the car is driving itself. At last they reach the building and turn in to the parking lot. "I don't think I've ever been here before," Loretta says, gazing up. They walk along the tree-lined path to the gray limestone building. Despite its dismal facade, the building is filled with large windows and light, which is what Andrea likes about it. "It's nicer inside," Andrea says, and they go in.

In the elevator, Andrea realizes just how shabby the place is. The elevator is large, the size of a small room, which is good for the artwork being transported in and out, but its gears make a groaning noise as it lifts them slowly. There is a smell of urine, which seems stronger than usual. Andrea thinks that one of the nighttime security guards, perhaps Garcia, the one who frightened her, might take a piss at the end of his shift in the elevator.

Graffiti is scrawled across the walls—"This building sucks," "Fuck me"—along with assorted phone numbers. This building bears no resemblance to the wood-paneled hallways of the Gothic structures that form the center of the campus. It has always seemed funky and offbeat to Andrea. Now it just looks shabby.

They stand side-by-side in the ride up, facing the doors. "No, I'm sure I haven't been here before. I'd remember this elevator," Loretta says with a laugh.

"Yes, I hadn't realized how memorable it is until now."

"I'd think you'd have art exhibits in the building."

"Oh, we do, but not for public consumption. They do that over in the library, when the college actually wants people to see it."

It is one of the things that has made Andrea angry with the college. No matter how many times she has asked, they have never allowed her to do an exhibit of student work at the library. It might set a precedent, the college replied, and then they'd have to allow all the art teachers and other faculty to use the exhibition space. The exhibition is used instead for traveling shows and faculty exhibits, and group shows once or twice a year.

Andrea has had her work in one or two of these exhibits. Never more than a few pieces. Usually in an exhibit of her peers at the year-end faculty show. But it was always a hodgepodge—a few abstracts by Jim Adler; artistic black-and-white photos taken around campus by the university photographer who runs the photo lab; a conceptual artist who works with string. Andrea always felt that her work needed to be seen in its totality for its cumulative effect, not mixed in with the works of others. The only way it could have its impact would be, as with her friend who made the sculptures of her mother's head, in a solo show.

The elevator doors open at last, and they walk down the gray corridor. Red paint splatters the walls. There is a blue imprint of a child's hand, and Andrea wonders which colleague allowed his or her kid to do that. She feels her heart beating quickly. As they make their way down the dimly lit corridor, Andrea feels suddenly exposed.

But they walk in and Andrea gazes around. She is struck by the walls, covered with the five-by-seven or eight-by-eleven miniatures she has done on canvas, on wood, on paper. A blast of golden sun pours in, filling the room, and Andrea is relieved because it is the best way to see her work—in the natural light, in the middle of the day.

"Oh my," Loretta says, at first shielding her pale eyes. Slowly she takes it all in—the sun cascading into the small room, the paintings hung all over the walls. She goes to the far end, which is the right place to start, and takes her time, going from painting to painting in silence.

"They're all the same," Andrea says, apologizing for what she does. "They even all have the same name."

"But they're different, too," Loretta replies, standing back to get a better look. "And they are very interesting." She studies them for a long moment. Then picks up a painting of the house in autumn, a family on the porch, a doll on the lawn, its arms and legs ripped off, the eyes in the head fallen back into the skull. "And quite disturbing. This one, it's as if the doll has been murdered."

"Yes, I suppose she has been. But the family has no idea . . . They're just eating their barbecue." Andrea gazes at the painting and nods. "I've got several with dolls," she says. She points to a dark corner on the canvas. "And a lot with this shadow."

"Whose shadow is it?" Loretta asks, staring closely.

"I'm not sure. Someone, or something, larger than life."

"Larger than life?" Loretta ponders this. "The perspective is interesting. Is this the front of the house? From the road?"

Andrea stands beside her. "Oh, no," she says. "You could never see the house from the road. It has a long driveway lined with trees. If no one told you, you wouldn't even know a house was there."

Loretta moves her gaze from image to image. "So you are painting it from the backyard?"

As Andrea thinks about this, she realizes that you could not get this view of the house from the backyard, either. You would have to be standing much farther back than that. "Actually, you can only get this vista on the lake, which is right here." She stands in front of one of the paintings, holding a pencil in midair where an imaginary boat would be.

Andrea wonders why this hasn't really occurred to her before.

Her father used to snap pictures of the house from their fishing boat all the time. It was the only place to see the house. Years later, when Andrea began her series, she painted from this vantage point— that of those early mornings with her father in the middle of the lake. A perspective she had when she was ten years old.

Though she began to paint the house on Shallow Lake series months ago, Andrea has not given much thought to the vantage point. She painted the house as a whole, low to the ground. But now she understands that the only place she could ever really see the house was from the middle of the lake. She paints from the place where the boy drowned.

In the elevator down, Loretta says, "Tell me about that house."

"It was my home," Andrea says. "It's a long story."

Loretta looks at her, expecting more.

"I'm not ready to go into this yet," Andrea says. Then they get in their cars and drive away.

Four

There is a French restaurant, a bistro in the mall, and Loretta is sitting at a table, glasses on, reading not the menu but a galley proof from a writer who wants her endorsement. As Andrea pulls up, she can see her concentrating. Andrea knows that Loretta has so many requests for blurbs, for speaking engagements. To talk to a group of schoolchildren in Harlem, to judge an emerging writers contest.

Loretta uses every spare moment in restaurants, in doctors' offices, at lectures, in this way. She carries a leather satchel filled with galleys, manuscripts, letters, and notecards. She can do only so much that people ask of her. Andrea has heard Loretta complain "I can't give everyone a quote, can I?"

Andrea checks her hair in the dashboard mirror, puts lipstick on, then rushes in. She is late, as usual. It is not out of rudeness or ambivalence, it's just the way she is. It has always bothered Andrea because her father was so punctual and she wants to be that way as well. But all her life she has been ten, fifteen minutes late, not late enough to make someone get up and walk out, but late enough to set the mood of the meal, to turn people off just slightly, to make everyone she is supposed to meet a little bit annoyed.

But Loretta doesn't seem angry at all. She is ensconced in the novel and doesn't notice Andrea when she walks in. She even seems startled. "I'm sorry," Andrea says, coming hastily to the table, carrying her own heavy bag of books and papers, which she flings on the extra chair. "I lost track of the time."

"Oh no, it's quite all right. I was just reading." Loretta takes off the granny glasses that rest on her nose. She puts down the galley, careful to dog-ear her place, and reaches up to give Andrea a hug. Andrea has worn a tailored brown jacket and slacks, an outfit that seems cobbled together to her, but it's the best she can do. The slacks are loose, and she realizes she has been forgetting to eat. Loretta is in a long black skirt that makes her look slightly matronly and a blue turtleneck that seems to be choking her. There are red marks around her throat. Her gray hair is pulled back, but strands fall around her face. She brushes them away with her hand.

"So." Loretta puts her reading glasses back on and picks up the menu. "What do you feel like?"

"I have no idea." Andrea feels inadequate to this moment. She is thinking about Greg, her most difficult student, with whom she missed an appointment today. She had called and asked the department secretary to leave a note on her door. She'd had to take Chief to the vet with a thorn in his paw. But when she checked her voice mail, Greg had left what Andrea had to think of as a hostile message. "Professor Geller, this is your student Greg Josephson, I believe we had an appointment . . ."

Glancing at the menu, Andrea is overwhelmed by the choices.

She isn't used to being dressed up, holding a menu in her hand. It is not that she hasn't done this before. She did it many times with her father and her mother, with her father and Elena. But she always felt out of place, as if she was playing a part. It never came comfortably to her. Not the way hiking boots and a down vest do.

"I like this place," Andrea says, looking around.

Loretta peers over her glasses. "You've been here before?"

"No, I just like it. I like the decor. I like the amber lights." Andrea takes a sip of ice water. She breaks off a piece of a seeded roll the waiter has just brought, then realizes she has taken the roll from Loretta's plate. "Oh, excuse me. I guess this is yours. I always make this mistake. Left, right."

"It's a form of brain damage," Loretta says.

Surprised, Andrea says, "What? Taking your bread?"

"No, the left/right confusion. I read it just the other day. It's brain damage."

Andrea looks troubled. "I can never tell right from left."

"Don't worry. Many people can't." The waiter, a young man with blond hair and blue eyes, comes by and offers to tell them the specials. Loretta listens, carefully inquiring about the ingredients in a certain sauce, whether a half-portion is available. Then, with the waiter still poised beside them, she turns to Andrea. "So what do you see?"

"I don't know. What are you going to have?"

Loretta peers into the menu. "Let's make this easy. Why don't we take a bottle of your Sancerre? You'll drink white, won't you?" she asks Andrea, who nods, understanding that Sancerre must be white wine. "And I think the arugula salad and the blackened salmon."

"That sounds good." Andrea closes her menu without really looking at it. "I'll have the same. If that's all right. Then I don't need to think about it."

"Of course that's all right." Loretta nods to the waiter, who listens attentively to the order, then slips away.

Andrea looks down sheepishly. "I've never been very decisive about the little things. What to wear, what to eat. I have trouble with those. But the big things . . ."

"You feel clearer about."

"Yes, I do. For example, I always knew I wanted to be an artist. I know where I like to live. I'm good at . . ." Andrea hesitates, looking for the right word. "Moral decisions. Maybe I don't do left and right very well," she goes on with a grin, "but I can do right and wrong."

"That's a good sense to have. A moral compass."

"That's true," Andrea agrees. "I have a good moral compass. And I'm very loyal, until—"

"Until what?"

"Until someone crosses me," Andrea says with a little laugh.

Loretta laughs as well. "And has someone crossed you lately?"

"Maybe." Andrea shrugs. "Someone has . . ." She gazes around. She finds the restaurant surprisingly restful. She likes the subdued colors—tangerine and mauve. She likes sitting here with Loretta, who can almost finish her sentences for her.

"And who gave you your moral compass? I've always had this feeling about children: someone saves them. Who saved you?"

Andrea hesitates, not saying anything. She wonders if Loretta is going to reveal something about herself and her relation to her own family. Perhaps even her son. She has never mentioned him.

It is an odd omission, Andrea thinks. Once or twice Andrea has thought of bringing him up, but she checks herself each time. The subject seems taboo. But then Loretta rarely speaks about herself at all. Somehow no matter what Loretta is talking about, it gets turned around, coiled on itself, and becomes about the other person. But Andrea doesn't mind. She is happy to have Loretta listen.

"Who saved me?" she asks.

Loretta nods. "Who helped you? Who gave you your sense of direction?"

Andrea laughs. "I'm not sure I've got a very good sense of direction." She thinks how easily she gets lost. It has always been one of her best excuses for being late.

"I don't mean literally."

"I suppose I have a strong sense of justice. That comes from my father. I think I got the important things from him."

Their salads arrive, and they pick up their forks, but neither takes a bite. "Like what?"

"He believed in hard work. He believed that a person should strive for what she wants. When I wanted something for myself, he made sure I got it. Like ice skating."

"Oh, I didn't know you skated."

"Yes, actually." Andrea blushes. "Well, I competed. For a brief time my brother and I skated pairs."

"A brother-and-sister team? Isn't that unusual?"

"Oh, not at all, not at the junior level. If brothers and sisters grow up skating together, as we did, they can train easily. We were very good. Our father hired an excellent coach."

Andrea smiles, thinking of her father. He would show up rinkside, shivering in his brown shearling coat, watching their three-turns. He kept a chart of their progress. There were eight different three-turns and he'd count them out on a clipboard: forward, right, outside edge. Backward, left, inside edge.

Andrea is enjoying this conversation. She relaxes and decides it is because Loretta seems truly interested, listening to every word as Andrea explains how she loved to skate and how her father gave her so many opportunities. "He threw himself into whatever we did. He learned what we wanted to learn. He relearned algebra just to help us with our homework."

Loretta frowns. "It almost sounds as if he might have been a little pushy."

Andrea bristles slightly. "No, not at all. He just wanted to be there for us. Really, he was my inspiration."

"Do you still skate?"

"I haven't in years."

Some people have come in and are seated at a table not far from them. Andrea notices that the woman is staring. Loretta looks up and smiles, giving the woman a nod.

"Do you know her?" Andrea asks and Loretta shrugs.

"I don't think so." Loretta leans forward, whispering into Andrea's ear. "People just seem to know who I am."

"How disconcerting."

"Yes, at times it makes me feel very strange. I often wonder where I know a person from when I don't even know him at all."

Andrea nods. "I can see where this would be unsettling."

"Once—this was very funny—I was in Iceland, and there was this native people's parade. Dancers in traditional costume and masks were prancing down the street and one of them in this huge mask, surrounded with feathers, came right up to me and said, 'Are you Loretta Partlow? I just love your books.' "

They both laugh, and the woman at the other table looks upset, as if they are laughing at her. But Loretta smiles graciously at the woman, who looks back at her menu.

"Where were we?" Loretta asks.

"Skating."

"Yes, why did you stop?" Loretta holds a fork poised in her hand, but her eyes are set on Andrea. Andrea expects that she will be interrupted, but Loretta just leans forward, not saying a word.

"I don't know. I lost interest in it, I guess. I mean, my parents divorced. My father had joint custody of us for a while. But we were always going back and forth, shuttling between my mother's house and his. At one point our parents even considered our staying in one house and their moving in and out. We were always leaving a book, a sweater, at one place or another. It just became so complicated."

Andrea is thinking that this doesn't have much to do with skating when she notices the waiter fluttering around them. It occurs to her that the waiter knows who Loretta is. He has a concerned look on his face. Their fish is ready, but neither has eaten much of their salad. With subtle expertise, Loretta moves her salad plate to the side so that the waiter can put down the main course. Andrea, without flinching or pausing to tell her story, does the same.

"And then what happened?" Loretta asks.

"He married Elena. No one knew much about her. She came from somewhere out west. She didn't seem to have any family. There wasn't a single person from her past at her wedding. She claimed she was an only child. Her parents were dead. It didn't occur to us then—we were little, after all—that she had left something behind. Somehow we just accepted this. At first she was very nice. She made great food. She was always baking cookies for us. She won us over."

Their fish is in front of them, blackened and dark, getting cold. The waiter looks worried, but Loretta gives him a smile. "Everything is fine," she says to him. Then to Andrea, "And then?"

"Well, very slowly, so we were hardly aware of it, Elena began isolating our father. Taking him further and further away from us, from his friends."

"How would she do that?"

Andrea takes her first bite of fish. It is spicy and burns her tongue. She puts her fork down. "Are you sure you want to hear this? I don't want to burden you."

"I am very sure."

"Well, it was subtle. At first it just seemed like they were busy when we were free. They had social engagements on nights when he was supposed to see us. We rarely saw him alone. Weekends when he knew we couldn't go with him, they went up to the lake. Oh, he'd invite us, but it was our soccer season or we had SATs. Things like that."

Andrea pauses, takes a sip of wine. She wants to be sure Loretta is still interested, and when Loretta nods for her to go on, Andrea continues, "Then she started having him go away with her. She'd book elaborate vacations over the holidays to surprise him. Then he'd be gone when we were free. She'd schedule things on the weekends we were to see him. It wasn't long before we hardly saw him at all. Before . . ." Andrea is looking for the right word.

"Before he became a stranger to us. Anyway, somewhere along the line, skating became irrelevant."

"I had no idea you had such a hard time."

Loretta's pale eyes are focused firmly on Andrea. She is concentrating on her as sharply as she would on any book. Andrea is struck with a sense that Loretta really is interested. That she does want to hear what she has to say. "Yes, it's true. Perhaps I shouldn't go on. It is an odd story, and I have no idea what you'll think." Andrea takes another bite of the salmon and decides it is too spicy to eat. She puts down her fork and sips her wine. "Anyway, we saw less and less of him. That house, the one I paint, we didn't go there anymore. In fact"—Andrea feels a swollen rage rising—"I haven't been there in years."

"I thought it was a place you went to often."

"Yes, before, I used to. But now it's just a place I remember." Andrea sighs, realizing how sad she is that this is true. "After a while he requested that joint custody stop. He said it wasn't sensible anymore. He was more well known, and they traveled a great deal. It had stopped for all practical purposes, but now he asked the court."

"That must have been very painful."

"Yes, it was. My brother, Robby, was furious, but I saw it differently. I assumed my father was happy and that Elena was doing what he wanted. He seemed happy, but we had no idea how alone he was. But we managed to stay close, to see one another as often as we could. In the last few years we spoke every day. Then he had his accident. And Elena began behaving oddly. One thing led to another . . ."

"What do you mean?" Loretta leans closer. She has hardly touched her food, either.

"I shouldn't be talking about this. I haven't told many people, but I want to talk to you. I feel as if we're getting to be friends."

"We are already friends," Loretta says, touching Andrea's arm. "And I am happy about that. All my friends are old and stodgy. You are young, easy to be with."

"Can I tell you something? I feel as if you would understand. It's very private, but I want to confide in you. You have to promise not to tell anyone."

Loretta nods slowly. "I promise; I won't tell a soul."

"Yes," Andrea says, "I think I can trust you."

She is ready to speak when their waiter returns. He asks about their food and if anything was wrong. They both reassure him that it was fine, but they weren't that hungry. They ask him to wrap up the meals so they can take them home.

The waiter hands their plates to the busboy. Then he scrapes the tablecloth with a small silver implement. Andrea watches as he does this meticulously, not missing a crumb. She wishes he would leave. Or that Loretta would think to send him away. But she does not, and when he is finished, he inquires, "Can I interest you ladies in dessert?"

"Oh, yes," Loretta says. "They have wonderful desserts here. I love the almond marble cake. Do you have that?"

The waiter frowns. "No, I'm sorry, we don't, but we have a walnut torte. I had a piece just before my shift, and I can tell you, it is fantastic."

"What else do you have?" Loretta is smiling up at him. Andrea feels a tightening in her chest. She is about to tell Loretta what she has told few people, but instead they are hearing the description of the chocolate pistachio crepe drizzled in raspberry sauce, the walnut orange cake, the medley of homemade sorbets. "Oh, those sound wonderful. What flavor are they?" Loretta asks.

"Let me check," the waiter says, scurrying away.

"Their sorbets are especially good," Loretta tells Andrea. "They're homemade."

Andrea watches the waiter disappear through the swinging kitchen doors. The doors make a flapping sound. There is a small voice in the back of Andrea's brain, telling her that she should say no more. There is some reason why she must not go on with this conversation. Then, like a character in some slapstick comedy, the waiter rushes through the swinging doors again, and they make the same flapping sound.

He returns, somewhat flushed, with the news: "Mango, coconut, and chocolate."

"I'll have that." Loretta says. "And some of those little cookies that you make. The lacy ones."

The waiter glances at Andrea, who shakes her head. Though there is hunger in the pit of her stomach, she says, "I can't eat any more."

"So," Loretta says, "where were we?"

"I'm not sure," Andrea replies.

"You were about to tell me something," Loretta says. "About your stepmother and her role in what happened to your father."

"Yes." Andrea takes a sip of her wine. She is relieved. Loretta has not lost the thread of the story. Her interest has not waned after all.

"I used to believe that my stepmother kept my father from us because she loved him and wanted him to herself. But I don't believe that anymore. I think she wanted him for herself so she could have everything."

"You mean his estate? His property?"

Andrea nods. "Yes. Everything."

The sorbets arrive in a bird's nest of pastry, looking like an Easter basket, with two spoons.

"Coffee?" the waiter asks as he puts the sorbets down.

Now Andrea does wave him away. She is ready to continue. "Maybe you don't want to hear this," she says to Loretta.

"Please, go on."

"You see—and this is the part that you can't tell anyone—some people will think I am crazy, but I don't believe my father just died. I think Elena wanted him dead. He was a man who should not have been driving. He was taking a delicate balance of sedating medications for his heart, for depression. I think she overmedicated him, and not that she caused the accident, but she knew he was impaired. And yet she sent him out that night. Or at least she let him go. She knew there was a chance . . ." Andrea had to catch her breath. "A chance he wouldn't make it home."

Loretta looks at her, a hand across her mouth. "Really . . . that's terrible. I mean, it's not murder, I guess, not exactly, but, well, it's something."

"Yes," Andrea says, "but apparently it's something you can never prove."

Even as she says it, Andrea wonders if this sounds right. But it does not matter, because through the salad and the main course, through the wine, most of which she herself consumed, into the dessert and coffee, Andrea seems to have tapped in to Loretta's infinite capacity to listen.

When dinner is over and they have their doggy bags, they fight over the bill, which Andrea can't afford anyway. Loretta wins. "Really, it's been my pleasure," she says, snatching it away. "Now you owe me."

It is still early when they leave the restaurant. Loretta invites Andrea back for a nightcap. "Just stop in for a moment. Patrick would love to see you." They drive home slowly, Loretta in the lead.

When they pull up, Patrick greets them both with his warm kiss and limp handshake. Andrea settles into the softness of the couch, which she has grown accustomed to. She knows she will sink only so far. "So, what would you like? Some port, cognac?" Patrick asks.

Andrea has already had too much to drink but agrees to a glass of port.

"How was dinner?"

Loretta looks at Andrea, then over at Patrick. "We had the salmon. It was too spicy, wasn't it? But we had a good time." She smiles at Andrea as they make small talk. Loretta is concerned about getting some bulbs she ordered into the ground. Patrick says he'll give the nursery a call in the morning. Andrea sips her port as Patrick and Loretta banter.

"I think it's too many bulbs. Every year it's the same thing," Patrick says. "It's too much work. Don't you think so?" he asks Andrea.

Andrea shrugs. "I love your garden in the spring. In every season."

"You can see our garden?" Patrick asks. "From the top floor of the Romanellis'? I wouldn't have thought you could."

Andrea pauses, thinking this through. In order to really see their garden, she does have to lean, but she doesn't want Patrick to know. "Yes, I have a good view from my bedroom window."

"Isn't the Warburtons' house in the way?"

"No, your house is higher than theirs. Your garden is beautiful, and I think Loretta should do whatever she likes about the bulbs."

"See." Loretta is pointing to Patrick. "See," she is repeating with a wifely tease when the phone rings. Loretta and Patrick look at each other and frown, then they both shrug. Loretta picks it up. She has a displeased look on her face as she whispers, "Just a minute." She glances at Patrick. And then to Andrea, "I'm going to get this in the kitchen."

There are gestures between husband and wife. Small tells. Andrea can see how put out Patrick is by this call; he knows it will upset his wife. Andrea can hear Loretta speaking in low, angry tones from the kitchen. There is something about money. A few moments later, she hangs up and comes back to them.

"Well," she says, "I'm sorry about that."

"Anything wrong?" Andrea asks.

Loretta waves her hand. "Oh no, just some publishing matter. Nothing at all." But there is a tightness to her mouth, a little pout.

Then Loretta says she is tired, and Andrea rises from the sofa. "I'd better be getting home," she says. Patrick walks her to the door, and she can see his concern.

"I hope nothing is wrong." She wants to ask if that was their son, then thinks better of it. But it occurs to her that these people have their problems, too.

"No, everything is just fine," Patrick says, then he shuts the door behind Andrea. Hours later, when she gets ready for bed, she sees that the lights at the Partlow home are still on. Slowly, one at a time, they are turned off. But a single light remains, and Andrea sits at her window, watching it burn.

One afternoon Gil shows up at Andrea's studio. They make love, but in daylight his face is craggy. His eyes are unkind. What is stranger to her is that he does not excite her. Not the way he always has. It is as if his movements are mechanical. And now she assumes they always have been. In the end she fakes her orgasm.

Later, as they are pulling their clothes on, he says, "So you never told me. Did you tell Loretta about your father? Did you say it was a secret?"

Andrea looks at him, perplexed. Briefly, she has forgotten her original purpose. "What do you mean?"

"You said you were going to tell Loretta your story in confidence. So that she would write about it."

Andrea shakes her head, realizing that her conversations with Loretta have taken on a life of their own. "Oh, no. I decided not to in the end."

"And why is that?"

"It just didn't seem relevant anymore."

"Well, I'm glad," he says. "I'm glad you feel that way." When he leaves, Andrea sits on her couch, staring at a blank canvas. After a while she gets up and suddenly starts to paint *The House on Shallow Lake #38* though she has not moved forward with her series in weeks.

She begins with the house on a brilliant fall day. She paints in colors she has never used before—sienna, burnt orange, ocher. A form begins to take shape. A face at the window. A silhouette, some-one Andrea has never seen. She knows this person has never been inside the house before, but she is glad the woman has appeared.

She paints until dawn. When she is done, she puts the painting on the floor, lies down on the sofa, and sleeps.

As the air becomes colder, Andrea thinks of skating. Even though she no longer skates, it comes back to her at this time of year. She moves like a skater. Her body makes small pivots, a shift of weight on a sharp blade. When she takes a break in her studio, she skates across the floor. As she executes a three-turn, a twirl, a waltz jump, a voice in her head says, "Stay on your edge. Shift your weight."

Her father stands at rinkside, his gloved hands folded across his chest. "Edges," he shouts. "It's all about edges."

His sport used to be golf. He would take Andrea and Robby to the driving range. Robby never liked to go. He thought golf was stupid—hitting that little ball into a little hole a million miles away—but Andrea liked it. Her father would take her to the driving range and buy her a bucket of balls. He taught her these things: head down. Eye on the ball. Follow through.

Lessons she has carried through life, though with varying degrees of success.

One Tuesday after her class, Andrea pulls into the library parking lot. She has some books to return, and she wants to look for some slides on three-dimensional objects. As she gets out, she notices some flyers taped to a lamppost. Andrea takes them all in at once. The top one reads: "Have you seen a white pigeon?" with a cell-phone number to call. The next reads: "Tex, you dog. Call me. Everyone else does. Jane." The third is a picture of Loretta's face, unsmiling, staring out at her.

It is a rather austere image, from one of Loretta's early book jackets, and it does not reflect the way she looks now. Andrea goes up to the flyer and reads, "I am a professor of contemporary litera-ture in Hungary, and I am trying to contact Loretta Partlow. I have a gift for her. I am in the country for two weeks. If anyone can help me, I will offer a reward." There is a cell-phone number and an e-mail address. Bemused, Andrea goes into the library, where there is another copy of this flyer on the bulletin board next to postings for roommates wanted and self-defense karate.

Later, when she goes to the diner in downtown Hartwood, Andrea sees the flyer taped to telephone poles, on store windows, on the back of the newspaper kiosk. It is in the grocery store and the coffee shop. Though the white pigeon and the message from Jane appear sporadically, this one is all over town. Andrea feels sad for the person who lost his pigeon and admires Jane's boldness. But she's troubled by the ones pertaining to Loretta, and she begins to take these down. She tears them off windows and poles.

She removes them from the bulletin boards and the kiosk. Then she drives to the library and rips the sign off the lamppost in the parking lot.

Probably the person is harmless, but Andrea is concerned. She keeps seeing these flyers around campus, and she continues to take them down. But more seem to appear whenever she removes one. Finally she has a large pile at home, neatly stacked. She thinks she should show them to Loretta and Patrick. They have invited her for drinks that evening, so she decides to bring them.

When Andrea walks in, Loretta is sitting on the couch, reading a book. A fire roars in the hearth. She looks so comfortable. She smiles at Andrea warmly, nothing like that face in the posters. Andrea thinks that if she had a place like this to sit, she'd never get up.

"I brought you these," she says, handing Patrick the envelope with the flyers. "I didn't know if I should."

Patrick opens the envelope and looks at the flyers. "Oh, not this guy. Is he at it again?"

"He says he has a gift for you," Andrea says to Loretta.

Loretta nods. "It's always the same thing. Books he has written in Hungarian. Usually he leaves them with the English department, but he still wants to meet me. You collected all of these?"

"They were all over town. You aren't afraid?"

"I'm sure he's perfectly harmless. People like this usually are, but it's better not to encourage them." Patrick crumples the flyers slowly and tosses them into the fire.

At Thanksgiving, Robby decides to fly out from San Francisco. "I haven't been home since the funeral," he says. Andrea realizes it is true. Though she has been out to see him once or twice, he has not been home. He did not even bother to come when the will was read. Or when it was contested. "It was pointless. I already knew." Robby has explained to Andrea that he moved past loss and anger into acceptance. "And poverty," he likes to quip. "It is what it is. I am not fighting it anymore." Robby tells Andrea he will arrive on Wednesday and spend the day with her; then they'll drive over to Montrose, where their mother will have a meal.

A week before Thanksgiving, on campus, Andrea runs into Loretta, who asks what her holiday plans are. "Oh, my brother is coming into town. We're going to our mother's."

"Oh, that's good," Loretta says. "Patrick and I were wondering if you wanted to have dinner with us, but I'm glad you have plans."

From the way Loretta says this, Andrea can see she is disappointed. "Are you having people over?" Andrea asks shyly.

"Well, we were thinking of it . . . I wanted to see what you were doing first."

"Why don't I call my mother? It will just be us and my mother's companion, Jack. I'm sure you'd be welcome."

"Oh, I don't want to inconvenience her."

"I'm sure that if my mother feels inconvenienced, she'll let me know."

"That would be lovely," Loretta says.

Andrea goes home, surprised. It had not occurred to her that Loretta would want to come to her mother's for the holiday, but it seems as if she does. When she calls her mother, Barbara is surprised as well. "Why would she want to have Thanksgiving with us? Doesn't she have dozens of people to be with?"

"I guess not," Andrea says. It occurs to her then that Loretta and Patrick have no family, no one with whom to share a holiday. "Maybe they have no one special."

"Well, I've never read anything," Barbara says. "Where should I begin?"

"Oh, it's all right," Andrea says. "She's not that kind of person. We've actually gotten to be good friends."

"You have?" Barbara asks.

Robby is also taken aback to hear that Loretta Partlow is coming to Thanksgiving dinner. His partner, Marty, who will not be coming, as he is going to see his family in Los Angeles, thinks the novelist is a goddess. When Andrea next calls Robby to firm up their plans, Marty grabs the phone. "Oh my God," Marty says, "is she really going to be there? I just love that novel about the man who eats his lover."

Marty actually debates changing his plans to come along. Andrea hears Robby in the background: "You can't do that to your family."

"She just *gets* gay culture. Do you know what I mean? She *gets* it," Marty says.

When Andrea picks Robby up at the airport, he looks fit and tanned. He's wearing a Gore-Tex jacket. "Very California," she says. She is also impressed that he has only a carry-on bag with him. "Is this it?" she asks, trying to lift it. "My God, Robby, what have you got in here? I thought you were traveling light."

Robby looks at her sheepishly. "Marty made me bring them." He unzips the bag, and inside she sees a half dozen or so of Loretta's books.

"You've got to be kidding."

"Oh, come on, Andrea. He's a huge fan."

Bullwinkle is on his back. One leg and antler float in the air. Big Bird hovers off the ground, and the helium technicians are struggling to keep the Pink Panther down. Robby loops his arm through Andrea's. "Oh my God," he says, "it's about to go."

They laugh as the crowd groans. Robby has insisted that they drive into the city to see them blowing up the parade balloons outside the American Museum of Natural History. It is a cold night, and Andrea didn't want to go, but Robby said, "We have to. I haven't been in years."

Once the Pink Panther is secured, they buy hot cider from a man selling it on the corner. They watch the men trying to tighten the cables around the Pink Panther. They move back to Bullwinkle, where Robby reads the blow-up instructions: "Left foot, right antler, right foot, left antler." "Boy, bummer if you've got dyslexia," Robby says.

The cold slaps their faces, and Robby twirls his sister around. "This is so great," Andrea says, shivering as she takes his arm. "Remember how we used to come here all the time?"

Robby smiles. "I remember once."

"No, we came a lot."

Robby is shaking his head in that skeptical way. "I don't think so . . ."

"You were little," Andrea says. "What would you know? It was all the time."

The leaves are turning—it is a blazing fall day as they head out to Montrose. Loretta and Patrick will come later. Before leaving, Andrea phoned to give Patrick very explicit directions. In the end she carried a map over to his house. He was busily making pumpkin pies to bring. He's fussy, she thought, like a woman. Or like her brother.

Andrea and Robby get to their mother's early. A good thing. Barbara is in her usual state—distracted, confused. Outside of the shopping and the martinis, Jack, Barbara's companion, has mixed, nothing has been done. Recipes lie around, including one for goose, which they aren't having. The turkey has not even been stuffed, let alone put in the oven. Robby does a quick calculation: thirteen pounds at twenty minutes a pound. "Okay," he says, using his hand as a walkie-talkie, "I need backup. Let's get this bird in."

Andrea rolls her eyes as he flexes his muscles. "Who's going to eat all that?" she asks.

"Oh, you'll be surprised."

Andrea and Robby move effortlessly in the kitchen, slicing potatoes, boiling cranberries. They learned to do this as children, negotiating their parents' households, fending for themselves. Robby is in charge of the creamed-spinach casserole, which he whips up with sticks of butter. Andrea will do the yams and the cranberries, as she always does. They slide around, touching each other on the waist, never bumping. It is what they learned from their years of skating together.

With the turkey in, Robby starts cutting strips of tinfoil. He makes a tinfoil bikini and briefly decorates the turkey with it. "What are you doing?" Andrea asks.

"It comes out looking like a bathing beauty."

"No way," Andrea says, ripping the tinfoil from his hands.

"Stop fighting, children," Barbara says, waving her hands. She is worried over the seating. She has carefully written out little cards. But where will everyone sit? Who sits next to whom?

"Mom, let them work it out. It will be fine," Andrea says.

"Is she left-handed? Should I put her on the end?"

"Who? Loretta? Yes, she is. Put her on the end."

Barbara is polishing silver, adjusting her grandmother's linen on the table. At four o'clock sharp, Loretta and Patrick arrive, having given themselves plenty of time. Patrick comes in with a pie in each hand. Loretta carries chocolates and flowers, a bouquet of autumnal blooms—the last from the garden, she says.

There are cocktails. Wine and some stronger. Jack, a retired businessman who has been with Barbara for the past five years, serves green-apple martinis in plaid pants and a red vest. "Can't you make him change those things?" she asks her mother.

"He looks like Santa's helper," Robby whispers into Andrea's ear. Then he greets Loretta, shaking her hand. "I'm so honored to meet you," he says.

"Well, I'm very happy to meet you as well."

There is half an hour of chitchat, mostly about the coming millennium. The discussion turns to Y2K. Patrick is concerned. "I think everything is going to come crashing down."

"Oh, it's nonsense," Loretta says. "It's just a hoax."

"But a hoax by whom?" Barbara asks.

"The computer-technology people. People who want the world to spend billions on this instead of feeding the poor."

"Well," Patrick says, "you might think so, but I'm moving everything out of the stock market."

Loretta rolls her eyes at him. "Survivalist," she hisses. Then Robby announces that dinner is served. It is a buffet of steaming platters—candied yams, sausage stuffing, a golden-brown turkey, the cranberries that haven't quite jelled, spinach casserole, whipped potatoes, a salad of Roquefort and pear, a wild-rice-and-mushroom dish that Robby just had to do, and Patrick's pumpkin pies. There are the appropriate admiring groans, a round of applause, then an eating frenzy begins. Plates piled high, once, twice. "This is delicious," Loretta says, and Patrick agrees.

"The children are so good at this," Barbara says, waving her hand.

Robby nods. "When you're raised by wolves . . ."

Andrea gives him a look, and he smiles at her, one of his knowing grins. Barbara sighs, shaking her head. "I can't even give him a compliment."

"It's all right, Mom." Andrea pats her mother on the arm. "Seconds, anyone?"

"This will be thirds for me," Loretta says. Andrea wonders again how she can eat so much and be so thin. Meals go right to Andrea's hips. She has to walk everything off.

Afterward, there is dessert in the living room, and coffee and cognac. Andrea helps clear while Robby follows Loretta, looking to corner her. He has brought the tote bag of books from the car, and when Andrea comes in with a tray of cream and sugar, she sees Loretta sitting on the sofa, the pile of her books at her feet, signing them all to "Robby and Marty."

"Oh, we just loved that one," Robby says, pointing to *What's Eating You*. "It's so twisted and funny. Yet so right . . . But I think this is my favorite." He holds up a tattered paperback of *Carnage*.

"Oh, that's so old," Loretta says.

"Our book group read it. You do soldiers so well."

Andrea places the tray on a sideboard and returns to the kitchen for the coffeepot, the cups, and saucers. When she carries the coffeepot back to the living room, the mood has shifted.

Pausing in the doorway, she sees Robby still sitting at Loretta's feet. The books have all been signed and put back into the bag. They are speaking softly, intimately, their heads bowed together. As Andrea hesitates, she overhears Loretta say, "Oh, yes, I know. I know how hard it's been. She was so close to him."

Andrea sees Robby pull back a little, raise an eyebrow. "You must be kidding. They didn't speak for years."

"Oh, but I thought—"

"I don't think so." Robby is pursing his lips when Andrea enters the room with the loaded tray. She glares at her brother, who jumps to his feet. "Can I help?"

She shakes her head. "No, I'm fine." But Robby pounces on the tray, taking it from her hands.

Later, when Andrea is in the kitchen, rinsing, drying dishes, scrubbing the counters clean, Loretta comes in. There is a clatter, the sound of dishes being stacked. Loretta picks up a cloth and begins wiping platters dry. She polishes them until she can see her reflection. "I didn't mean to be prying," she says, leaning close to Andrea, near the sink.

"It's all right. My brother just talks."

Loretta is carefully drying a platter, checking it before she puts it down. "But you didn't tell me you didn't speak to your father for years."

"It wasn't for years." Andrea shakes her head. "And it wasn't a big deal. Not really. You know, it was an adolescent thing. We were always close."

"But you had a break . . ."

Andrea reaches into the soapy water, pulling the plug. A sucking sound comes from the drain. "It was just a hiatus. Just a little while." With a brush, she scrubs the sink.

"Your brother implied—"

Andrea shakes her head. "My brother is a drama queen. He gets everything wrong." She takes the cloth Loretta has been using and wipes her hands. "There," she says, "I think we're done."

On the car ride home, Andrea is barely speaking to Robby. He fiddles with the radio, trying to get a pop station. "I thought she was nice. Your friend."

"She is nice."

"She's not like her books. I thought she'd be mean and standoffish, but she isn't at all."

"No, I said she wasn't." Andrea drives with her eyes fixed to the road.

"What's wrong with you? You're kinda quiet."

Andrea sighs. "It wasn't great, you know, to say what you said about me and Dad. I don't need you telling stories about me."

Robby gives her a shocked expression. "I'm not telling her stories. She asked. She was curious about you. Anyway, it's true, isn't it? You and Dad didn't speak for years."

"No, it's not true. Maybe there were times, weeks, but certainly not years. You remember it your way, and I remember it mine. Just like with the balloons."

As she pulls into the driveway, she hears her dogs barking. "Well, what way was it?" Robby asks.

"We were never out of touch. You were younger. You just remember what you want to remember. Or what you were told." She storms out of the car and climbs the stairs with Robby trailing behind. "We didn't see him as often because of Elena, because they traveled a lot, because of the way she was. But he was always in our lives. He was always there." After she clomps into and out of the house with the dogs, Robby chases her into the night.

"Then why are you so pissed off?" Robby shouts. "Because you know it wasn't just Elena. It was him, too." But she is slipping out of sight, past the Warburtons' and Vitales', to the path near the Partlows' house. She hears him as she disappears into the woods. "Andrea," he calls. Then fainter, "Andrea."

She keeps walking. He had no business telling Loretta things about her that weren't true. Or saying the things he said. She is furious with Robby and sorry she invited him to visit. He was always rather shallow, only seeing things from a narrow point of view.

It is dark and cold in the woods, and the dogs aren't used to being there at night. They don't race ahead in the moonlight, but stay close to her side. When Andrea gets to the pond, she sees that it is lightly frozen over. The moon reflects on it, and a mist rises from the surface. She puts a foot on it, hears it crack. For a moment she contemplates testing it, walking out farther. But she knows this is a foolish thought. Besides, she doesn't want her dogs to run on it. Already she is cold, so she whistles for them to follow her home.

When they return, Robby is sitting on the porch in one of her parkas, waiting for her. He has made coffee. He gazes at her with his big gray eyes. "I'm sorry," he says. "I didn't mean to give away any family secrets."

"You didn't give away any secrets. You misrepresented what happened. I don't know what Loretta will think." Andrea feels frightened at that thought. Then she decides she is being silly. She will explain everything to Loretta, who will think nothing of it at all.

She pats her brother on the head and takes the coffee out of his hands. She sits beside him and drinks from his cup. "It's all right," she says. "You didn't mean it. You didn't do any harm."

He wraps his arm around her. "I wish I could help you."

"Help me with what?" She brushes his arm away.

"Nothing," he says, recoiling. "I don't know."

Before he leaves for San Francisco, Robby spends his last night going through the albums and drawers of pictures Andrea has tucked away. She rarely gets them out, but because he asks, because he wants to see them, she does. He spends the better part of the evening sipping wine, pointing, laughing at photos of them in a bathtub, on a raft. In matching hula skirts. "Shades of things to come," he says. He wants to take some home. "To show the shrink," he says.

When he leaves, Andrea drives him to the Albany airport. He gives her a crushing hug, tells her to come see him soon. When he disappears beyond airport security, she heads home. It is late when she gets back, and she makes herself some dinner, has a glass or two of wine. The photo albums sit on the table, and Andrea leafs through, casually at first, as she might with a newspaper.

Some of the pictures are just loose, never put away. But others are in labeled albums of journeys, family vacations. The Grand Canyon. Cycling through the Loire. There isn't much past then. She sees her mother, stuck in time, long dark hair falling across her shoulders, in summer dresses with spaghetti straps, a hand on each child's arm. Her parents, cycling side by side, waving at the camera.

How did we get from there to here? She wonders, turning pages. There is one trip without the children. A Caribbean cruise. Barbara has carefully marked the head of this page: "Our Getaway." Now she sees her parents as she never has before. Lounging in deck chairs. Dining at the captain's table. It was a mystery cruise and Barbara has kept the program, with a Sherlock Holmes hat and pipe design on the front; she has circled the Agatha Christie lecture series.

Andrea flips through, then looks more carefully. It is as if she is in the library, scrutinizing slides of the female body. She begins scanning each picture with greater care. She is looking for something, but she doesn't know what. Over and over she flips through the pictures of the cruise—her mother laughing, holding Simon's hand. Simon stealing a kiss. The two of them dancing.

Andrea puts the albums away and gets in bed, but the dogs keep scratching. Pablo has a dog dream and shakes in his sleep. She can't sleep anyway. She thinks of popping an Ambien, but instead gets up and puts the light on, goes back to the albums. Something is bothering her. She can't name it, but she knows it is there. She knows it caught her eye. She takes a bright reading light and puts it on the coffee table, then begins going through the few pages of cruise pictures again.

One after another, she examines the shots. And then she sees it. A picture of her parents, taken against the railing, arms entwined. But someone else—a woman seated in the background—is caught in the corner, just slipping out of the frame. Seated in a chair. Her head turned as she tried to look away but doesn't quite succeed. There she is. Andrea recognizes her right away.

She begins calling Robby frantically and reaches him as he just walks in. "My God," he says, "give me time to put my suitcase down."

"Robby," Andrea says, "I was looking at the album. The cruise Mom and Dad took—a long time ago."

"And?"

"And Elena is in one of the pictures. She was there. She must have gone on that cruise. I can't believe it."

"Oh, I really doubt it . . ."

"She's in the picture," Andrea says.

Robby pauses. "So they were seeing each other. So he was a cad. I'm not sure why it keeps surprising you. But it doesn't surprise me."

"But she planned it. She planned everything."

"She planned some things, Andrea." She can hear Robby sighing, weary from his journey, tired of the whole thing. "But it doesn't mean she killed him."

"But she's that kind of a person."

"So? Lots of people are."

Andrea's doorbell rings a few days later, and she sees Loretta standing on the porch, wearing one of her polar-fleece running suits, a pink one that Andrea thinks isn't very flattering. Loretta's arms are laden with books. Andrea gives a shout: "I'll be right down."

Loretta calls back, "I brought you a few things."

Andrea panics at the thought of Loretta coming up to her apartment. She hasn't straightened up since Robby left. There are dishes in the sink. The bed is unmade, the floors are filthy with kibble that has rolled out of the dog dishes, the chairs covered with dog hair.

There are piles of clutter everywhere. Even Robby has said, "I don't see how you can live like this."

She makes a cursory effort, tossing the Indian-print spread over the bed, dumping papers off the chairs. She rushes out to the landing in time to see Mrs. Romanelli intercepting Loretta on the stairs.

"Oh," Mrs. Romanelli says, wiping her hands on her apron, "I was making some soup. I saw you standing on the porch. I thought you must be here for Andrea, but I wasn't sure if she was home."

Andrea sees Loretta's eyes widen in a startled look. "I was just dropping these off," Loretta says, looking up at Andrea, who is now bounding down the stairs.

"It's all right, Mrs. Romanelli," Andrea shouts, "I'm here."

Mrs. Romanelli reaches out with a wrinkled hand that smells of flour, touching Loretta's sleeve. "You're the writer, aren't you?"

Loretta jumps back in a skittish way. Like a horse that hasn't been broken. A feral cat. It is definitely an animal move. A cornered animal. Mrs. Romanelli takes a step back, then shakes her head, slipping into her rooms.

"Here," Loretta says, her voice annoyed by the encounter with the landlady. "I brought you these. Some novels I wanted to loan you, and a few books of art history I thought you might like. People send me these things all the time. I just don't have room for them anymore."

"Oh, you shouldn't have. Would you like to come inside?"

"No, I have so much to do. But we wanted to thank you for having us to your mother's. Here." She foists the books into Andrea's arms. "You can keep the art books. I'm just heading off to the library." Before Andrea can say anything more, Loretta is out the door.

Later that evening, as Andrea is leaving for her studio, Mrs. Romanelli catches her at the door. "What's wrong with your friend?" she asks. She shakes her head. "You better not touch her."

For several days Andrea does not see or speak with Loretta. Then late one afternoon Loretta calls. She is sorry she hasn't phoned sooner. "We are just so busy. We were just deciding about this trip to Argentina . . ."

Andrea says, "I know what you mean." Even though she doesn't. She has no idea what it means to be busy the way this woman is busy. To have demands on your time, people who want to see you, invite you to their colleges to speak, give blurbs to their books, read for their literary prizes, and so on. To be asked to go to China and Argentina. To be able to say no. A million things to do all the time. All the accoutrements of success.

What was it her father used to tell her? "Make people think you are a success. Always put on a good face." And her mother always seconded it. "If you have the dress, you'll have the occasion." They did not mean act the part. They meant *be* the part.

"Patrick is in the city tonight. Some Literary Guild event. I don't know. He's on the board."

"Well," Andrea says hesitantly, "would you like to have dinner? Or would you like to come over and I'll buy you a drink?" Andrea likes that expression—"buy you a drink"—though she is surprised to hear it come from her own lips. It is what rich, urbane people say. Grown-ups. "Let me buy you a drink." Andrea likes the fact that she can sound this way. As though she is a busy person with things to do—a person who can buy other people drinks.

But of course there is no drink to buy. There isn't even any wine or beer. She has nothing in the house. Andrea has been trying to quit drinking. Or at least cut back. Not keep it at home. She's been drinking alone when it's around. She doesn't think she handles it very well.

When Loretta says yes, Andrea does a quick calculation in her head. She'll have to get to the ATM, the store. She'll have to straighten up. She is figuring out how much time and money she needs when Loretta says, "A drink would be nice. What time would be convenient for you, Andrea?"

"Oh, say around seven."

Suddenly Andrea is excited. She is also wondering if she can do all the things she has to do before seven o'clock. And whether she has enough money in the bank, which she may not. First she takes the dogs out for a run, then locks them in the apartment. On her way out, she knocks on Mrs. Romanelli's door. Not wanting a repeat of the other day, she says, "My friend is coming over. The novelist. Just so you know, she'll be here at seven, so you don't have to open the door."

Mrs. Romanelli shakes her head. "Don't worry. I won't be opening the door for her."

On the way to the store, Andrea thinks about what she should get. What would Loretta drink? Campari and soda? Isn't that what writers like? Or just white wine. Andrea doesn't know that much about wine. Most of the drinking she's done in her life has been done in bars. Or Scotch at night, alone.

When she's expecting company, she usually purchases a pear-shaped bottle of Mateus, the kind every college student buys. She's bought a large bottle of merlot for a few parties, but it's not what she does. She doesn't know what people like. Sweet or dry. Red or white.

She will assume white and dry.

At the mall Andrea pulls in and rushes into the grocery store, where she purchases seltzer and orange juice. She buys a wedge of Brie, some gourmet olives, frozen cheese puffs, frozen mushroom caps. Then she dashes to the liquor store, where the shelves are labeled by country—France, Italy, Spain, California. As a painter, she decides to go by the labels. She looks for one with a nice painting: distant mountains, vineyards, elegant script.

She grabs a Riesling that has mountains and a stream on the label (she likes the drawing) and hurries home. It is almost six. She puts the wine in the freezer and the frozen tidbits and mushroom caps on a cookie sheet. Then she throws her bed together, vacuums the floor. She Dustbusts the chairs and turns over the cushions she can't get clean.

After examining the table, she tosses a cloth over it to cover the water and paint stains, the dog-chewed legs. She grabs the dog toys and hurls them in a closet. She gets on her knees with paper towels and scrubs the linoleum in front of the kitchen sink. She pours disinfectant into the toilet, drags the mildewed shower curtain closed to cover up the rust-stained bathtub, then scents the whole apartment with a lemony spray.

Rifling through her CDs, she comes up with a few choices. She puts on Coltrane. She lights some scented candles—sandalwood, cinnamon, rose. She hopes they will neutralize the smell of wet dog. Looking around, Andrea thinks the place looks presentable enough. Then she settles down and waits.

Loretta arrives an hour late. She apologizes. "It's not like me at all. I got so caught up in my work. It almost never happens. You should have called me. I lost track of the time." She pauses, taking a deep breath. "This is very charming, Andrea. You've made a cozy nest for yourself."

On the dining room table Andrea has put out a spread—the Brie and the olives, the Carr's crackers nicely displayed on a circular platter. She has just pulled the tidbits and cheese puffs out of the oven, and these, too, she has arranged in a checkerboard arrangement. "You have a lovely visual sense," Loretta says, "even in arranging hors d'oeuvres." She pops a cheese puff into her mouth, then makes a fanning motion with her hand. "Hot," she says. Andrea rushes to the sink and gets a glass of tap water, but Loretta waves her away.

Andrea has forgotten about the wine in the freezer, but now she remembers. When she takes it out, there is a chunk of ice like a frozen heart in the center of the bottle.

"How did you get that in there?" Loretta says, laughing.

Andrea looks at her, confused. "I put the bottle in the freezer."

"I know, I know," Loretta says, laughing gently. "I was just teasing you. It's like a boat in a bottle. It's rather pretty, isn't it? A frozen heart."

Andrea has some difficulty uncorking the wine, then pours it into two glass tumblers (she has no wineglasses, she remembered when she returned home). Loretta takes a sip. "Oh," she says, her face shaping itself into a pout. "Demi-sec."

Andrea looks at her, then at the bottle, not entirely sure what "demi-sec" means, but she sees it written on the bottle. She takes a sip of the wine, which is sweet, syrupy. "I'm sorry. I thought it was dry."

Loretta waves it away. "It doesn't make any difference. This is just fine."

With the glass in her hand, Loretta walks around the small apartment, gazing at the pictures on the walls, the books. Andrea realizes to her dismay that she has by her bedside many of the novels by Loretta Partlow, but Loretta doesn't seem to notice these. Instead she fixates on the photograph of the house on Shallow Lake. "So this is the house? The one you paint?"

"Yes," Andrea says, standing beside Loretta so they can look at it together. "It was our country house. But it is the place I call home."

"I can see why. It is very beautiful. And you can only see it from this perspective, from the middle of the lake, right?"

"Right," Andrea says.

"Who took the picture?"

Andrea shrugs. "My father, I believe. A long time ago." She is not sure who took it, but she remembers that day. A fried-chicken lunch, all of them fishing. Her mother saying something simple and her father laughing. It is the last time she can remember the four of them together.

When Andrea pulls her gaze away from the picture, she sees that Loretta has gone to the window. She is holding back the curtain with one hand and twisting her body so she can look out. Andrea comes to stand beside her. "So," Loretta says, looking down, "this is what the view is like from here."

Gazing down, Andrea sees the road, the garden, and Loretta's house. Beyond that she can see the woods and the pond. The one light on between Andrea's room and the woods is in Loretta's studio. Andrea half expects to see Loretta there.

Loretta looks at her, her brow furrowed. "Do you see me when I am working?"

Andrea shrugs. "Sometimes I can see you," she says, "but mostly it's just your shadow or silhouette. It's not really you."

Loretta seems satisfied with this answer. "It's a little odd for me to think about you up here, looking down at me."

"I don't really do that . . ."

Loretta laughs. "Of course you do. Everyone does." She lets go of the curtain. "At least I know what I look like from up here." She slumps into the sofa, and Chief nuzzles his snout in her crotch. She swats the dog away, a harder swat than needed, Andrea thinks.

"No, Chief, bad dog," Andrea says. "Go in the corner." She yanks the dog by his collar, tugs him off. He goes and sulks on his bed. Then Andrea and Loretta sit, legs curled beneath them, and talk for a few moments about the college, work. "You know, I can't get out of my head what you told me at the bistro. It's such a disturbing story," Loretta says, putting her glass on the coffee table beside the hors d'oeuvres she has not touched. "It almost makes no sense."

Andrea is relieved that Loretta has not mentioned what Robby told her. Perhaps she understands that was a private matter—the kind of thing that happens when families fall apart—and that it did not concern her. Besides, it happened when Andrea was very young. "No, its parts don't. But if you add them up, they do. Why was he driving that night? Why didn't she ever go to the hospital? Why did she sell everything? Where did she come from? Where did she go? I can't get these questions out of my head."

Loretta's eyes blink like a slot machine as Andrea rattles off the questions. Andrea has a strange sense that Loretta is memorizing everything she says. "Anyway, it's never added up. He had no business being on that road, let alone driving. And I'm sure she was overmedicating him. He seemed confused, disoriented, right before the end."

Loretta brushes a strand of gray hair off her face. "But they had been together for years."

"Yes, over ten years. I'm not saying it was always like this . . . And she never did anything specific, anything that I would call hurtful. I believed he was happy. It didn't surprise me that he left everything to her. But it did surprise me when she disappeared."

"But murder . . ."

Andrea flushes, uncertain. "I wouldn't exactly call it murder. Let's just say that a man taking the doses of medication he was should not have been driving no matter what. I have a feeling, because he did seem so confused in the last few days before the accident, that she was overmedicating him. Perhaps to keep him quiet. He had gotten temperamental in the last few months."

Loretta leans forward, her face resting in her palms. "Was she just a gold digger? I mean, ten years is a long time to be a gold digger."

"At first I didn't know what to think. They *were* married for many years. I was disturbed when he had the accident, but I didn't suspect anything until afterward. She seemed so put out. I started to think that she wanted to get rid of him. He had become a burden to her. He was cramping her style. It became like a puzzle. A lot of little pieces that slowly fit together."

"Such as?"

Andrea's heart is beating quickly, and she is having some trouble catching her breath. "Elena didn't seem to care about him or the accident. It was a big inconvenience to her, I think, that he didn't die right away. Once she actually said so. She said that since the accident, she'd had so much to do. So much paperwork. She could hardly do things for herself, like go to the gym or get her nails done. She really said that. And she looked great after the accident, completely unfazed."

Loretta shakes her head, making a "tsk" noise with her lips. "Where do you think he was going that night?"

Andrea shrugs. "I have no idea."

There is a pause. Andrea can hear the Romanellis' TV downstairs. She hears her dogs' heavy breathing. Outside, a cold wind blows through the trees. Loretta reaches across and pats Andrea's hand, holding it lightly in her own. "My God, you've been through so much."

Andrea nods. "I suppose I have."

They sit silently, Loretta's hand still resting on Andrea's. They are both startled by the sound of a car screeching past the house. Loretta sits up as if waking from a dream. She goes to the window. "Oh, that must be Patrick. He drives too fast. He's home early. I should go, but come for dinner in the next day or so. I'll give you a call." Loretta gives Andrea a hug, a quick kiss on the cheek. Andrea listens to her footsteps on the stairs. She gazes out and sees Loretta, racing down the sidewalk to her house, where Patrick has just pulled in. Then Andrea sits down at the table where the neat platters of the Brie, the olives, the crackers lie. The bottle of wine, barely touched, its frozen heart now melted, stands open. Andrea pours herself a large glass, which she sips. It is warm and sweeter than before.

The hors d'oeuvres, now cold, remain in their checkerboard pattern. Andrea pretends to play checkers, moving a cheese puff across the imaginary board. Though she knows she shouldn't, she sips more wine, pouring until the bottle is done. Realizing she is ravenous, Andrea eats until it's late, then falls into bed.

Five

Today the assignment in life drawing is the parts. "We are not doing the whole body," Andrea tells them. "Just look at the forms. The angle of a wrist, a thigh, the curve of the spine. I want you to sit very close to the model. Use a pencil. Ten minutes, then switch parts."

It gives Andrea pleasure to see her class learning to draw. Drawing is her touchstone; it is the way she judges any artist. Jackson Pollock said once that if he hadn't learned to draw trees, he never would have moved into abstract. Andrea believes that anyone can learn. It is just a matter of seeing.

She stops at the chair of one particularly ordinary student and notices that he has drawn an arm in quick, deft strokes. "Switch poses," she says to the model, and the student looks up at her, bereft.

She picks up the charcoal and draws sharp lines, like hieroglyphics, holding the page up for the class to see. "Now do a leg." And to the model, "Keep moving."

After class, Andrea heads over to the faculty house for high tea. Natalie and Patty are waiting for her. "Long time no see," Natalie says, giving her a wave. Andrea has just made herself comfortable, nestling into a leather armchair near her friends, when Loretta stops by. "Andrea," she says with a big smile. "I never run into you here."

Loretta carries her leather satchel, a pile of books in her arms. She wears her big red coat and glasses. There is an extra seat beside Andrea where coats and book bags have been piled, and the young women quickly move them out of the way so Loretta can settle herself into the soft leather chair. The other two girls stare at her. A living legend. A national treasure. And she knows Andrea well enough to sit down to tea.

"Loretta, these are my friends. This is Patty." Loretta turns to Patty. "And this is my friend Natalie. She's a violinist."

Loretta extends her hand to Natalie, and as the two clasp hands, Loretta holds on to Natalie's fingers a moment longer. She lets the white fingers slide out of her grasp slowly. "You have beautiful hands," Loretta says, holding them in her own, still looking at them. "I've always wanted to play the violin. I've heard it's the most difficult instrument of all."

Natalie nods. "It is very difficult, but I've been playing since I was a little girl."

"She was a prodigy," Andrea says.

Loretta nods, impressed. "I never get to meet the junior faculty.

You are always so interesting. You have so much more going on than we do." She notices the case by Natalie's side. "Is that your violin?"

Natalie nods and reaches for it. "Here. You can look."

Natalie unsnaps the case, and they all peer down at the shiny red violin. She takes it out and hands the instrument to Loretta, who cradles it nervously, as someone might who has never held a child. Natalie lets Loretta feel the weight, the smooth cherry wood, the bow. Then Natalie lifts the instrument to her chin and pretends to play. While they anticipate music, she plays silently for a few moments, an impassioned musical mime, then takes an exaggerated bow.

Loretta claps when the imaginary performance is done. Then she gets up to leave. "I'd love to hear you play something besides silence the next time," Loretta says. Gathering her things, turning to Andrea, she says, "I'm sure I'll see you very soon."

That weekend Andrea has some of the books Loretta lent her. They have taken to swapping—big thick art books, mostly on women painters Loretta admires: Lee Krasner, Joan Mitchell, Helen Frankenthaler. Andrea has developed the habit of not calling. Of just stopping in.

It is an unseasonably warm day, and Andrea leaves home without a jacket. She'd say there was a hint of spring, not winter, just ahead. The mums have remained hardy, and Andrea pauses to admire them. Then she rings the bell.

As usual, Patrick answers. He is such a big, ruddy man. Somewhat overbearing. Andrea doesn't like the way he breathes heavily.

It occurs to her that she can hear him breathing like her dogs. "You know," he says, seeming happier than she has ever seen him, "Loretta is working . . ." His body fills the doorway like a bouncer's.

"Oh, that's good. I don't want to interrupt."

"No," he says, smiling. "Maybe I can help you?"

Andrea smiles back with the sense that she is intruding. She understands Patrick. Since the day he met Loretta thirty-five years ago, he has known what his role would be. It has never been in doubt. It is to protect her, so she may do what she was put on the planet to do. He has never questioned it and he has never balked. That would have been unthinkable. Patrick has never asked more of Loretta than she is willing to give. And he is always there in his job as her enabler. In this way, he has been the perfect husband.

They met in a class at Iowa. It is a well-documented anecdote he has talked about in interviews. He remembers it perfectly—"Chastity and Desire in the Eighteenth Century." A bizarre course that consisted mainly of reading love letters, epistolary novels, and the fiction of unknown female writers. It was a tedious academic exercise by anyone's standards, except Loretta, who was consumed by the material. It was in their first conversation that she said to him, "I think it is amazing. I never thought of this. How chastity gives birth to desire. It is the unattainable we long for. That is human psychology, isn't it?"

And Patrick had agreed, not because he really agreed, or because he'd even thought about it very much, but because she spoke with such earnestness and authority. She had looked at him with her pale blue eyes and said, "It makes sense. We always want what we can't or shouldn't have."

They had been together ever since, first as friends and study partners, as readers and editors for each other, and briefly, in their marriage—enough to conceive one child—as lovers, though this was the least powerful part of what was between them. "The physical," Loretta once wrote, "can never be as compelling as the mind."

But she had supported him in his work. His novels—he had published three, to minor acclaim and some financial success—were dark urban tales, vaguely of crime, but mostly of psychological terror. Maniacs, perverts, stalkers: those weird psychological criminals were his domain, an interest she came to share.

As Loretta's success grew, Patrick had to apply his knowledge of stalkers to their own life. Such as the Hungarian man with his posters and his gift. There were those strange fans, the twins, who showed up at every reading, no matter where it was. They dressed alike, carried identical tote bags containing the same number of copies of each of Loretta's novels that they wished to have signed. Their names were Gwen and Glenna. They used to switch the order in which they came up to Loretta so that she would point to one and say, "You're Gwen, right?" The twin would reply with a sly smile, "No, I'm Glenna."

And there was that handsome boy who attached himself to Loretta after his mother's death. He told Loretta, "You look just like my mother. And she was the most beautiful woman in the world." Loretta had been flattered and drawn to him until the boy sent her a picture of his mother—a dowdy, matronly woman without any particular charm.

Patrick had had to protect Loretta from these people and more. He had had to protect her from herself. From her moods. Her doubts. Her little "dips," as she called them, into depression. The elevator going down. A kind of cavern she could topple into from which no one could retrieve her. She had suffered from nightmares of being buried alive, of being dropped into a dark hole from which there was no escape.

It occurs to Andrea as Patrick fills the doorway that perhaps he feels the need to protect Loretta from her—as if she were a stalker. Andrea knows this is absurd. But there is something in the way his body seems to block the door, the way he places himself between her and Loretta.

"Just tell her I stopped by. And thank her for loaning me these."

At first Andrea is troubled by her encounter with Patrick. It had never occurred to her, though now it clearly does, how easily he could stonewall her visits. Stand in the way of their contact. But slowly she forgets about it. It drifts into memory—"a bad moment," Andrea starts to think of it as.

Almost daily Loretta stops in to drop something off, to borrow something back. These exchanges have become part of the fabric of Andrea's life. They are frequent, spontaneous, though she tends to go unannounced to Loretta's less than Loretta comes to her. Still at any moment Andrea might get a call, an e-mail. "Come for a drink." "Are you free for a walk?" It is so easy, drifting back and forth from one house to the other.

Often Loretta comes up for tea, a chat. Andrea has taken to keeping Bengal Spice Celestial Seasonings in the house and some Walkers shortbread cookies, Loretta's favorite. Andrea keeps her place neater. Every day she makes her bed, hangs up her clothes, in case Loretta decides to pop in. And Andrea feels more comfortable stopping in on Loretta. Patrick seems less of a sentinel. He gives her a kiss on the cheek when he sees her, then shouts for Loretta: "Honey, your friend is here." It is rare when Loretta doesn't come right to the door.

Andrea can't help feeling as if Patrick has been scolded for keeping her out. But it is all forgiven, in the past. Loretta invites Andrea to her parties. Her "little gatherings," she calls them. She invites young men who work in departments such as Far Eastern languages and medieval history. They seem to be brought just for Andrea, so she talks to them about their courses. Once or twice they have called, asked her to dinner. Loretta has provided a social life for her, a kind she had not quite imagined before.

Almost daily there is something to talk about, a thought, a word. "Did you read that piece I sent you on Joseph Cornell? What did you think?" "Do you have any sugar? I can't bear running to the store." Andrea is not surprised when the phone rings one Saturday and it is Loretta asking for ideas for Patrick's birthday. "I have to get something for his sixtieth and I haven't got a clue."

"What does he need?"

"He doesn't need anything. That's the problem."

"Well, what does he want?"

Loretta laughs. "He never wants anything. He always says, 'I have a wallet. I have a sweater.' Men are so hard to shop for."

"Then get him a matador's cape. A bowling ball. Get him a boxed set of rap CDs. Something he'd never get himself."

"I can see Patrick in a matador's cape." Loretta is laughing. "But I should get him something like an oil-operated generator. He's threatening to build a bunker before the millennium. Anyway, I'll have to go to the mall."

"Why don't we go together?" Andrea says. "We could have lunch, figure something out he'd like."

"That's a wonderful idea."

At noon Andrea pulls into Loretta's driveway and gives a honk. In the doorway Loretta kisses Patrick on the cheek, then races out, wearing a blue parka and jeans. She looks younger, Andrea thinks, less dowdy. There's a lightness to her step. On the way they chat about life, birthdays, how silly men are, the upcoming millennium. All the Y2K concerns. "Patrick is completely worried, but I think it's ridiculous," Loretta says. "It's just news hype to give computer techies work. Nothing bad will happen."

"You really don't think so?"

"No, I feel very optimistic about the future," Loretta says. "About what lies ahead."

"Yes," Andrea says, smiling, "I suppose I do, too."

The mall is just a mile or so from Hartwood, but the drive is lovely, along tree-lined streets. As soon as they get there, Andrea knows the trip was a mistake. The huge parking lot is already packed, and they have to drive around looking for a space. It is, after all, not that many shopping days until Christmas. And there are the Y2K shoppers stockpiling batteries, bottled water, generators, canned goods. Andrea and Loretta get stuck behind a man driving home a small shed.

The mall is generic, with the usual Staples, Gap, and Old Navy. But it also has some of the more upscale stores, such as Brooks Brothers, J. Crew, and Burberry. They browse through Burberry first, laughing at the new line of doggy raincoats and leashes ("Kippy wouldn't be caught dead," Loretta quips). After less than an hour Loretta announces she's starving.

They head to the food court, where Loretta gets a Caesar salad and Andrea, surprised by how hungry she feels, goes for a Philly cheesesteak. As they eat, Loretta looks pale, exhausted. "This all feels pointless. What about a new pen? That might be nice. I could get his name engraved."

"That would make it more personal," Andrea says. "But doesn't he have pens?" After lunch and hours spent wandering through men's departments, fondling wallets and belts, dipping fountain pens into inkwells, looking at shirts and ties, considering a yellow cashmere vest, then deciding against all of it because nothing "feels right," the two women collapse on a bench beside a potted palm. "I give up," Loretta says. "I can't find a thing I like."

A fountain trickles in front of them, and two children stop to toss coins in. Their mother is arranging her packages on a bench nearby. Overhead, Muzak plays jazz standards. Rubbing her ankles, Andrea concurs that their mission has been unsuccessful. They watch the children, a boy and a girl—probably brother and sister—laughing, then fighting over the coins. The boy tosses a penny that misses the fountain and lands at Loretta's feet. Without thinking, Loretta throws the penny into the fountain, and the little girl starts to wail. "Oh, God," Loretta says, putting her hand over her ears. "Here," she calls to the children and fills their hands with coins.

"Say thank you to the lady," their mother says. "Say thank you."

Soon the children are laughing and tossing coins into the fountain again. Loretta yawns. "I need a coffee." They head over to Starbucks, and Andrea orders a skim decaf latte. Loretta has a chai. As they sit, sipping their drinks, Loretta rubs her brow. "I am really out of ideas." Then her face lights up. She turns to Andrea. "I don't know why I didn't think of this before. Why don't I buy one of your paintings for Patrick? It would be so personal. Nothing here appeals to me. This would be a gift that has some meaning."

"I don't know. They aren't really—"

"No," Loretta protests, waving her arms. "They are very interesting. He would love to have one."

"Are you sure?"

"Of course I am."

As they leave the mall, the sky is darkening. It looks like snow, the first of the season, and as they drive to Andrea's studio, it starts to flurry. She drives quickly, her wipers on. Though a gray sadness of winter hangs over their heads, Andrea doesn't mind. At her building, they take the elevator up, and Andrea flicks on the light. The studio feels warm and smells of fresh paint.

Loretta walks around slowly, finger to her mouth. Then she gets on her knees. Andrea is surprised by how agile she is, easily sinking to the floor. There she continues to study the paintings. She picks one up, then sets it down; then she lifts up one of Andrea's favorites, the most recent one—the house in winter, a version from memory, an idealized picture with a doll on the snowy lawn, its arms and legs torn off and lying at its side, and a faint figure at the window.

"You know," Loretta says, "these are all very haunting. I can't get them out of my mind. But I think this is the one he'd like. Here." She grabs it off the floor. "Who is this? In the window?"

Andrea shakes her head. "I have no idea. She just appeared rather late in the series."

"She looks like she's wearing a mask."

Andrea stares at her own work. "I think she is."

Loretta holds the painting out with her arms straight. "How much for this?"

Andrea shakes her head, trying to imagine giving this painting to someone for his birthday. She also doesn't know if she's ready to break up her series. If she ever wants to. "I don't know . . . I haven't sold—"

Loretta takes out her checkbook and writes a check for a thousand dollars. "Here. Will this do?"

Andrea stares at the check. "Oh yes, but it's too . . ."

But Loretta is holding the painting up in the air again. "This is perfect. It's haunting, really. Patrick will love it."

It is to be a surprise. Loretta mulls it over, but in the end she decides. "Don't you think it will be fun? A surprise party?"

"They never work," Andrea says. They are raking leaves, putting armfuls into black trash bags.

"But this one will, because Patrick is oblivious. He never knows what's going on. I'm going to have him playing squash with Doug Tramer. I'll tell him to be home by seven so we can go out for dinner. Then they'll come back and everyone will be here. What do you say?"

Andrea takes a pile of leaves in her rake and places them around the perennial bed. "I think it will be fun," she says, happy to be included in the planning. "If it works. I'll help you."

But Loretta doesn't need help. Gourmet to Go will cater. Student employment will provide a bartender, waiters. "We do this all the time," she says.

Andrea is excited by the prospect of this party. The provost, Doug Tramer, will be there. She has never actually met him, though they have been in a room together. And other important people—heads of departments, literary and artistic people from around Hartwood, those with no university affiliation but who are known all the same. And there will be her painting on the wall for everyone to see.

She envisions Loretta introducing her: "And this is our neighbor. No, our friend, Andrea. She painted that interesting picture on the wall." "Oh, you must see her work. Here we have one in the den." Andrea imagines the artists and writers, the renowned scholars from the college, stopping and gazing, admiring her work. Perhaps inquiring as to her technique, her subject. It could only help her standing in the community.

"Reach for the stars," her father would say. "You may never get there, but at least you've tried." He would have told her that this is a good thing. A break she needs.

She invites Charlie over one evening as she agonizes over what to wear. She has taken all her good clothes out of the closet. "What about this?" she asks, trying on a red dress.

He shakes his head. "Wrong decade."

She tosses it aside and reaches for a black skirt with a top. None of it seems right. "You need to go shopping," he tells her.

For the first time in a while, Andrea has money in the bank. She can afford something new. Together they go to the mall, where she tries on cocktail dresses that seem too fancy, too chic, and others that are too somber. She comes out of the dressing room, and

Charlie gives her a thumbs-up or thumbs-down. When she emerges in a simple black dress with spaghetti straps, Charlie applauds. "Bravo," he says. She'll drape a purple shawl over her arms. Let her hair down with two clips on the side.

At six-thirty, when Andrea walks in with Charlie, who has agreed to be her date for the night, a crowd is already gathering in the dim-lit living room. Andrea and Charlie are among the few who did not have to drive. All the other guests have been instructed to carpool and leave their cars in a wooded area on the left-hand side of the road outside Hartwood Springs. A student is there to greet them, take their keys, and direct them to the house. Patrick is due at seven. He will be coming from the opposite direction, and in the dark he will not be able to see the cars parked by the side of the road.

Andrea is nervous in crowds. She clutches Charlie by the arm as he leads her inside. She knows several of the people who are already here, but her eyes are on the walls. She moves through the room, wondering where Loretta has hung her painting. She steals glances down a corridor, then looks back at the guests in the room.

The Vitales from across the road are laughing with Gil and his wife, Lila, a poet with bad teeth who is known for her strident fem-inist lyrics. Gil gives Andrea a nod, then steers Lila into the living room, toward the bar. Jim Adler and his wife both kiss Andrea on the cheek. "I'm going to stop by your studio. Loretta tells me your new paintings are amazing," Jim says before being dragged away by his wife.

Of course their son is not there. Andrea thinks about this. It would be the kind of occasion a child would come home for, wouldn't it? Wouldn't you return for your father's sixtieth? But no one seems to notice. For all practical purposes, the boy, who is by now a man, has ceased to exist.

A student in a white shirt and black pants is walking around with a tray of champagne glasses, which guests grab. Another student comes by with squares of goat cheese on toast, sizzling mushroom caps. In the living room there is a spread—ham with honey-mustard dressing and roast beef with horseradish sauce, au gratin potatoes, a green bean and portobello dish, sun-dried tomatoes on mozzarella circles, and a Roquefort-endive salad.

Andrea feels queasy. She has already had a glass of wine that has gone to her head. She needs something in her stomach. As another waiter, a young male student Andrea has seen around campus, passes a tray of sushi on a bed of black olives, she reaches for a piece, dipping it in the sauce.

As an afterthought, she takes one of the olives as well, popping it in her mouth. Except it is not an olive. It is a stone. The waiter looks at her oddly, and Andrea, with the polished stone in her mouth, smiles at him as if this is their little joke. Inside her mouth the stone is smooth and cold. When he walks away, she spits it into her palm, then slips it in the base of a ficus plant near the French doors.

Scanning the walls, she is still looking for her picture. She thought Loretta would put it in the living room, perhaps off the side, near the bookcase. Or in the entryway, where there are other paintings of similar size. But she has not seen hers so far. She is about to wander down a wing off to the side where the studies and bathrooms are when she hears Loretta say in a loud whisper, "He's here. Quick, everyone in the living room."

They are all huddled in the dark in the living room. Andrea can feel the tension in the room, the excitement of bodies pressed against one another on this soft carpeting, champagne glasses clinking in their hands, a buzz of excitement. She glances at the ficus plant, wondering if anyone saw her bury the stone.

In a moment Patrick will walk in, and everyone will say, "Surprise." She is a part of this. For the time being, she forgets about her painting and where Loretta might have hung it. Instead she thinks how easily she fits in here. Never mind that she mistook a polished stone for an olive. She belongs to this group, this occasion. She has been invited. She is one of those people who will bring a fruit salad to the Partlows' on Labor Day, who will pick up an ornament for their tree whenever she is abroad.

There is some small talk, chatter. She hears Loretta say, "Oh, darling, you're early, and you're—" everyone hears Loretta hesitate—"wet."

Patrick replies, "Well, since we were going out, I thought I'd come home—"

On cue, a light is flicked on, and the roomful of people shout, "Surprise, surprise."

Patrick is standing there ruddy-faced and sweaty in his shorts and soaked T-shirt, a squash racquet in his hand. Doug Tramer stands beside him, likewise in his shorts and sweaty. The provost shrugs as Patrick breaks into a hearty laugh. "My God," Loretta says mournfully. "I thought you'd shower . . . It never occurred to me."

Doug Tramer shakes his head, laughing. "So did I. But he's stubborn."

"I don't believe this," Patrick says with a hearty laugh, good-natured. "No wonder you wanted me to shower. But it made more sense, since we were going to dress for dinner, not to dress twice."

Doug Tramer is still shaking his head. "I really tried, Loretta."

But Loretta is laughing a big, good-hearted laugh. "Happy birthday, darling." Her face looks luminous, delighted with the joke as she gives him air kisses on his sweaty cheeks.

All during the meal Andrea tries to balance a wineglass and a food plate at the same time. As she stands, poised, trying not to drop one thing or another, she catches snippets of conversation. Antonio Vitale is telling a small group, "So I went to the doctor, and I said, 'Doctor, that estrogen cream you gave my wife is working, but why is my voice changing?' " There is a titter. Andrea laughs with the rest of them, though she is not completely sure she gets it.

Someone says, "That one will be on the Internet before long."

"You can put it in the oral history of oral sex," Doug Tramer, who is also a historian, quips. Charlie is across the room, talking with one of the deans about the cost of computer preparation for Y2K, so Andrea returns to the buffet, where she eats like an animal rarely fed. She fills her plate again and again with roast beef, cheese, crudites, potatoes with a crispy cheese crust. She keeps looking for excuses to wander into different rooms in search of her painting, which doesn't seem to be hanging anywhere.

She'd assumed it would be. It has been over a week since Loretta purchased it. Wouldn't she want to put it up? To have it hanging for this occasion? Of course, it would be in Patrick's office. Ostensibly in search of a bathroom, she heads toward one of the dark corridors, but she finds herself in a corridor of closed doors. Trying to head back to the living room, she realizes she has oriented herself wrong. Though she has been in this house dozens of times, she has never been down the wings. From her window the offices look to be off to the left, but inside the house she needs to turn right.

She walks down another arm of the house. It is like a maze. Here the doors are open. There is a den lined with books, with a TV. All the guests' coats lie neatly across a daybed. Andrea passes the bedroom. Besides the canopied double bed with a green quilt, there are mahogany nightstands piled with books and a Tiffany reading lamp on either side. A big pile of reading pillows.

Andrea tries to envision Patrick and Loretta side by side in this bed, but she cannot. She wonders if this room is for show and there is another bedroom hidden somewhere. Next to the bedroom is an office, which she assumes must be Patrick's. Peering in, she sees a leather chair, a dark-wood desk. Again more books, manuscripts, all over the floor. Above the desk is a poster from the Frankfurt book fair, but that is all.

Andrea moves methodically from room to room, searching. She cannot understand why her picture is not in plain view. Then she realizes: it is his present. So Loretta will be giving it to him with the cake, when the gifts are opened. As Andrea moves between rooms, she searches for a wrapped rectangular gift and finds none. But it must be hidden in a closet. At any moment it will appear.

She is still in the corridor when Patrick appears. "Andrea," he says, surprised to find her here. "Are you lost?"

"I think I am. I was looking for the bathroom."

He makes a great flourish, directing her toward the living room, which has a powder room painted cranberry and rose, off to the side. Since Andrea is in the bathroom, she decides to pee. She sits down on the cold toilet seat (why are bathrooms so cold? she wonders), then washes her hands. The bathroom smells of potpourri and pine aerosol.

As she freshens up, she looks at herself in the mirror. Her face looks pale, almost sickly. She hopes the dark circles under her eyes are from the overhead lighting. Gazing into the three-way mirror, she sees herself reflected a dozen, a hundred times. Images of herself going back into infinity.

When she returns to the living room, she thinks perhaps she has had too much to drink. As she walks back into the room, she passes Gil Marken standing with Lila. They are having a heated discussion with Jim Adler. She tries to imagine how Gil can be married to that woman with her crooked teeth, her round, almost squat body. She can't imagine Gil with her at all.

Jim Adler with his thick gray beard, his hair falling around the side of his head, catches Andrea as she walks by. All he needs is a trident and he would be Poseidon. She has no choice but to join them. "The problem with this college," Gil is saying, "is the endowment. If we had money, we wouldn't have to answer to every student's complaint."

"It's all about privilege," Lila replies.

"I don't know." Jim stares at his feet. "I don't think we should blame the students. The administration has allowed this pattern of behavior."

"We should ask Tramer. See what he thinks," Gil says.

"Look, if we had a president who was raising money . . ."

Andrea, who normally avoids these kinds of discussions, pipes up. "I agree with Gil. My students go to the dean whenever anything goes wrong."

"I didn't know your students complained about you, Andrea," Jim teases.

"I don't mean often; I just mean they feel as if they can."

"Yes, entitled. That's exactly my point," Gil agrees. Lila Marken, who hadn't seemed to notice Andrea before glares at her, then looks away. When Charlie comes by with a plateful of food, Andrea is relieved to slip off.

"How are you doing?" he asks. He is eating roast beef between two pieces of French bread. "Holding up all right?"

"I don't know. Not so well, I think. My painting isn't here."

"What do you mean?"

"My painting. The one she bought for Patrick. It's just not here."

"Oh." Charlie looks around. "It must be somewhere."

Andrea shakes her head. "I don't see it anywhere." Just then the cake, aglow with candles, is wheeled out. It is in the shape of a squash racquet, and there is a knowing laugh as the lights are dimmed. They all burst into song, then the lights come back on and everyone blinks.

On top of the cake is an edible photograph of Patrick, with a big smile on his face, blond-haired, blue-eyed, from his sixth birthday. "Well, that is cute," says Doug Tramer's wife, Marissa. Everyone applauds as Patrick blows out his six candles. "Because really, you are like a six-year-old," Loretta says, making her toast. "And now we all get to eat Patrick."

Charlie is still looking around. He comes back to Andrea and says, "It's probably with the other gifts." Andrea nods, thinking that sounds reasonable, then notices the gifts piled on a sideboard.

There aren't that many. And those that are there aren't very large. They look like books and CDs and gift certificates. But there is no painting. And it was the reason why, Andrea realizes when it is not anywhere to be found, that she was so looking forward to this party.

While cake, coffee, and dessert drinks are served, Loretta makes an announcement, pointing to the sideboard. "We aren't going to open these gifts, because we said 'No gifts,' so we're just going to pretend all this isn't sitting here . . . for now."

"I feel like a kid at Christmas," Patrick says, beaming.

Andrea tries to let go of her disappointment, but it seems to be spreading like a rash. Inhabiting her entire body. She feels it creeping down her arms, her legs, as if it could choke the life out of her. It never occurred to her that her painting would not be in full view. It seems to her that Loretta should say something, but she does not. Andrea feels herself trapped in conversations, making small talk. A headache is beginning between her brows. She is trying to remember if she has any aspirin at home.

Charlie moves up beside her, looping his arm through hers. "You could ask her," he says.

"How can I?"

"Just ask where it is."

When the waiter passes a tray of sweet Sauternes, Andrea takes a glass and drinks it quickly. "Hey," Charlie says, "that stuff can go to your head." But it already has. Already Andrea is humiliated for trying to eat a stone and not seeing her painting. She does not want to ask, but she isn't sure how she can go home, how she can go to sleep and get up the next day without knowing why her painting, which Loretta bought for this occasion, is not on the wall for all to see.

Later, as people are gathering their coats and making their way to the door, as they are all congratulating Loretta on a great party and a great time, Andrea manages to ask, "You know, I was just wondering about the painting. I didn't see it . . ."

Loretta looks puzzled at first, then chagrined. "Of course, I should have said something, but I just forgot, with so many people and all the excitement. Yes, I was wrong not to mention it. Patrick loves it, but we're having it reframed. It will be ready next week."

"You should have told me," Andrea says, feeling foolish for having even brought it up, for having allowed it to spoil her good time. "I would have taken care of that for you."

"Oh, no, dear," Loretta says, "you have better things to do." With a wave of her hand, she turns to say goodbye to her other guests as they head out the door.

A few days later, Loretta calls and says, "Come to dinner, but you must help me cook."

"I'd love to," Andrea says.

She arrives at five, and the first thing Loretta does is steer her into Patrick's office, where he is on the phone, his e-mail displayed in front of him. "Look," Loretta says, pointing above Patrick's desk.

Andrea looks up and gasps. Right in the center of the office is her painting. "Just back from the framer. He loves it," Loretta tells her, "he really does."

Patrick, who is still on the phone, gives Andrea a thumbs-up.

"It looks good in its new frame," Andrea says, though the thin black frame doesn't look that different from the old one. "But it's a rather disturbing image, isn't it, to have floating above your desk?" She notices the gray outline where another picture recently hung.

"Not to Patrick. He finds it powerful. And you know Patrick is a very good judge."

They go to the kitchen where the long butcher-block table is covered with tomatoes and basil, peppers and red onion. There's an eggplant and winter squash. "Here," Loretta says, "you chop. I need a sous chef for this."

"Do you cook like this every night?" Andrea says.

"Not every night, but I love to cook." Loretta uncorks a bottle of white wine and pours two glasses. "You know what they say about writers and chefs. How we are the same people. We love to draw from life, from what's available, then we combine our ingredients, we concoct. And we don't always know what the outcome will be . . . Cooking, gardening, writing, painting. It's all the same thing."

Andrea laughs. "I never thought of it that way."

Miles Davis is playing on a CD player as Andrea chops. She has been handed a big carving knife and told to dice everything. She begins with the onion, the mushrooms. It is a soothing feeling—the big sharp knife, the cutting board. The smells of cooking.

Andrea keeps chopping. "So if a famous person were to paint you, someone from any time in history, who would you want it to be?"

"What a funny question." Loretta pauses from the salad she is tossing. "Vermeer. Yes, you've read my essay. I think Vermeer, because he captures a moment. He tells a story, doesn't he? And you?"

Andrea pauses, thinking it through. "Picasso. Because he sees the pieces of a person. He breaks down the whole."

Loretta nods, taking this in. An odd feeling of contentment, of belonging, starts to come over Andrea. It is as if she is easing herself down into warm water. She loses herself in the motion of her knife. She wants to stay here with these two people in this house, reading their books, chopping vegetables. She wants to be a daughter again. As she thinks this, she pauses, taking a sip of wine. Tears start to stream down her face. "What is it, my dear?" Loretta asks.

"I wish I could say it's the onion." Andrea laughs. Loretta looks at her, concerned, puts a hand on her wrist. "It's just that I haven't felt this normal in such a long time—being in someone's house, making dinner. It's been so long."

"It doesn't have to be so long again. We can do this anytime, whenever you like."

They have finished dicing the vegetables and now Loretta puts the linguine in a pot. There is a meaty sauce, which she stirs. "Oh, you know, I love to make sauces in the late summer, when the tomatoes and peppers are ripe, then have them in the winter."

"Yes," Andrea says, making a mental note. This is what people with fulfilling lives do. They dice vegetables on a cutting board, they make seasonal sauces and freeze them. They open distinctive bottles of wine.

Just before they sit down to eat, the phone rings. Patrick checks the caller ID and gives Loretta one of those looks. Loretta shakes her head, and they let the machine pick up. Andrea hears a young man's voice say, "Hi, it's me," before Loretta gets up and turns off the sound. Andrea can tell it is a lengthy message, because a long time passes before the blinking light comes on.

When the meal is ready, Patrick uncorks another bottle of wine.

This time a Bordeaux. Andrea watches as Loretta eats not one but two heaping bowls of pasta. She has never seen a woman eat so much. Andrea can barely finish what is in front of her. "You can eat so much?" she says. "You're lucky."

"Oh," Loretta says with a laugh, "I just burn it all off."

They finish dinner with a blueberry pie Patrick has made, "from blueberries we picked right outside our door." The pie is delicious. Andrea can taste the woody flavor, the creamy blueberry texture, the buttery crust. "I think this is the best meal I have ever had," she says, and they laugh, telling her she is sweet to say so.

"No, I mean it, it is."

"You are very kind, dear."

When the meal is over and the dishes are cleared, they sit in the living room, their feet up on the coffee table, lingering over coffee. From where Andrea sits, she can easily see the picture of their son—a handsome boy with dark eyes. She can also see the red blinking light on the answering machine.

When the time is right, she will ask. But not yet. Not now. At some point it will be right and they will want her to know.

Loretta yawns, and Andrea yawns, too. "They are infectious, aren't they?" Loretta says. Then she rises and Andrea knows it is time to leave. Andrea says good night and Loretta gives her a big hug before sending her home. It is a cold night. Andrea walks slowly, watching her breath form clouds.

It is late when she phones Charlie to tell him that her painting is now hanging on the wall. "I'm glad for you, Andrea," Charlie says in a sleepy voice. Andrea remembers that about him. His sleepy voice before bed.

"It looks good in her house," she tells him.

"I'm sure it does."

She is tempted to invite him over. To ask him to come stay with her. But she doesn't know what that would lead to. She doesn't know what she wants. Instead she says, "Their son. You babysat for him once?"

"Yeah, Sean. Sad kid."

"How so?"

Charlie sighs. "I don't know. He just seemed lonely to me."

"He calls once in a while."

"I'm not sure what's become of him," Charlie says. "I heard he got in trouble with some gambling debts. I don't think they see him anymore."

"I'm sure there are reasons on both ends."

"I'm sure there are." Charlie yawns. "Is that it, Andrea? Is that all?"

Andrea thinks there should be more, but in fact there isn't. "Yes, I just wanted to tell you that my painting is up."

"Well, I am glad about that, Andrea. I really am."

That night Andrea can't sleep. She lies in bed thinking of all the important people who pass through Loretta and Patrick Partlow's house. The visiting dignitaries, the writers from abroad, the political activists. Loretta knows at least two Nobel laureates, including a Peace Prize winner. All of these people will come to Loretta's house.

They will get a house tour. They will see Andrea's painting hanging above Patrick's desk.

Though she remains disappointed that the painting was not up for Patrick's birthday, that the provost did not see it or the senior colleagues from the visual-arts program, she knows that that picture will have other opportunities. People will come for holiday parties and birthdays and "paybacks" and parties just because one wants to have people over. Because one feels "in a party mood." "We do this all the time," Loretta had said.

Andrea envisions the guests asking, "Who painted that?" And Loretta replying, "Oh, our friend Andrea. She lives next door. I think she's very good." Andrea can imagine them asking if there are more where that one came from. Friends have bought paintings from her before, and of course her father and Robby and a few old boyfriends, and once in a while a collector will make a studio visit, but never someone like Loretta. Artists have had patrons for centuries, haven't they? Why couldn't Loretta wind up being hers?

Why couldn't she be even more than a patron?

Andrea knows this is strange, but her mind wanders to the boy named Sean. Now she knows his name. And he would not be a boy anymore. He would be, what, thirty, thirty-two? About her age. She tries to imagine him. Medium height, perhaps a bit bookish. Or dark with tattoos. A person on the edge. He might play with a rock band, ring through his nose, and he's on the outs with his parents because of drugs, money. All of the above.

If he ever came for a visit, Loretta would want to introduce her. He would need a friend. Andrea imagines a walk near the pond, long talks. They would have things in common—art, estrangement, Loretta. What if they liked each other? What if they became lovers?

What if they married? Andrea knows this is a huge leap, but it could happen. Stranger things have. What if they did? Then Loretta and Patrick would be her in-laws. This thought is extremely pleasing to Andrea. They would be family. She and Sean would go there for Thanksgiving, for Christmas. She couldn't always rely on Robby, after all, and certainly not on her mother. She would have a place to go on holidays.

There would be actual events, not makeshift meals. No more wondering whom to spend a holiday with. How to get through the day.

"I need to clean out my closets," Loretta says. "I've got so much junk."

Andrea is sitting in her kitchen, having tea. "Why don't we do it together? I hate doing those things alone."

"That's a great idea," Loretta says. "Come help me."

Together they trudge down the arm of the house where the den and the bedrooms are. They walk into the bedroom which is meticulous, not a paper anywhere, though there are piles of books on each bedstand, and they go into a room that is as large as Andrea's sleeping alcove. She realizes this is Loretta's closet. "My God," Andrea says.

"You see the problem. These California Closets. They're great, but you can accumulate so much junk."

Loretta begins pulling sweaters and skirts off shelves and hangers. She holds them up to her. "What do you think? Will I ever wear this again?"

Andrea starts rifling through the closet as well. She pulls down old corduroys, straight skirts, flowery dresses. "Time to get rid of these." They begin to make a pile on the bed.

"You know," Loretta says, "maybe you'd like some. Not the dresses or pants, of course, but the sweaters, the blouses. You could wear those."

"Oh, I don't think so."

"Why not?" Loretta holds up a cashmere turtleneck. "This is perfectly nice."

"It is," Andrea says, touching the green fabric. "Yes, well, if you don't want it . . ."

"I'm never going to wear half this stuff again. Here, and what about this? This would be lovely with your eyes."

Andrea slips on an aqua turtleneck that fits her very well. The fabric is so soft. She loves the feel of it against her skin. "I'll take whatever you don't want," Andrea says, and Loretta starts to make her a pile on the bed. When they are finished, there is more than Andrea can carry. "Really, it is too much."

But Loretta is folding the clothing, stuffing it into shopping bags. "I'm happy for you to have these."

When she gets home, Andrea places the sweaters on her bed. They are perfectly good sweaters. She folds them carefully and slips them into her drawers.

Andrea stays up late rereading the "unauthorized biography," the one that Loretta tried hard to stop. It is an odd compilation of unattributed quotes, anonymous anecdotes, and hypothetical scenes, reenacted. "A pack of lies," Patrick has said. Still, Andrea has found it useful. She has begun to piece together the truth about

Loretta and her son. It is in her stories—in one way or another.

It is clear from everything Andrea can glean that Loretta considered having a child an inconvenience that brought her slightly more trouble and less pleasure than a dog. In some of her stories, parents were forced to attend miserable school plays—those endless Greek sagas written by the English teacher, who, of course, longs to be a writer and corners the protagonist, often a writer, every chance he gets, asking if she could just look at his horrid retelling of Oedipus, the sanitized version of Medea slaying her children. Loretta herself sat through the plays, the recitals, the graduation processionals, the parent-teacher conferences—all the while with her little notepad open, scribbling the next scene for a story, the next line of a poem.

Motherhood had not transformed her the way everyone said it would. In the biography, a teacher who remained nameless described how Sean used to tug at Loretta's arm. "Mommy, are you listening? Mommy, are you there?" After a performance he'd say, "What did you think of me as the Artful Dodger?" and she'd look at him blankly. She hadn't seen him at all.

Being his mother was just an appendage, a neighbor claims. A small part of who Loretta was, what she did. It didn't pluck at her heart strings the way it did for other women. It didn't pull her apart. "In this aspect of her life, but in this aspect alone, she considered herself a failure," the biographer concluded.

Those poignant separations—the first day at school, seeing a sweet child head off with his backpack, the first overnight, summer camp—the little reminders that children are born to leave us, they were a relief to Loretta. It was one less thing she had to do, one more way she could concentrate, throw herself into her work, the one thing that mattered, that pushed her along, that made her what people thought of her, unstoppable, and what people made fun of her for.

And reviewers did make fun of her. Andrea cringes as she reads how one referred to her as "LP," as in "long-playing," a record that goes on and on. It was true; she had published so much. So many stories and novels that often seemed to go on and on (in serious need of cutting, critics said), plays and poems, essays and screenplays. Such a body of work for such a little woman. That was another thing people made fun of. She was so tiny, diminutive. When she and Patrick were first together, he could pick her up and carry her around the room.

Loretta had been called a furnace that must be fed. Housekeeping analogies had been applied to her. She was a sponge, a washerwoman of words. A black widow. There were caricatures of her—a madwoman, eyeballs popping out of her head, typing away. Her work was loved and hated, but she did not care. She was honored and revered, but often she was scorned. She rarely read her reviews. She used to—that was how she knew she had been called names, but now, she never looks at them. Patrick reads them instead. He keeps the good ones in a folder, so that when Loretta's emotional dips happen, those tumbles into a dark place, he can pull them out and show her. "See? Look what people say about you."

But if people knew the truth, the truth that Loretta Partlow does not want them to know, if she told them what she'd been through, they'd feel sorry for her, too. She doesn't want them to know. Because she lives with this dread—that if she tells anyone the truth, the engine will stop. The way she fears it almost has.

She rarely gives interviews. And if she does, she will discuss only the work. Never her life. "It is not relevant to what I do," she has said. But one critic has speculated that in recent years Loretta Partlow has begun to suffer from writer's block. Though this is not what Loretta would call it. She would say that for now she is taking a break. A pause. A hiatus.

Anyone can see that her head is full of stories. Her journals and notebooks, her scribbled pads and shreds of napkins, her boxes and files overflow with ideas. She has a dozen or more folders labeled "Misc." Still no story has taken hold of her in a long time. If anyone asks, she says she is looking for the right one to tell. But some suspect that for the past few years Loretta Partlow hasn't written a word.

This has been the only part of motherhood that may have come as a surprise. That since Sean has been gone, Loretta can think of nothing to say. When her son was little, she never stopped. She waited for those maternal feelings to kick in, but they never did. Though it seemed they had now. Loretta came to a kind of grinding halt, inexplicable really, though not entirely so.

She did not think, could not believe that what happened to her son was enough to bring her to a halt. She never believed that motherhood meant that much to her. That it would ever matter to her. But it seems as if it had.

Now, when Andrea gazes down from her window at Loretta, even late into the night, she sees that single light burning. A beacon of hope that brings Andrea great satisfaction. Because Loretta is working again.

Just before the winter break Andrea runs into Gil. He is cutting across campus on his way to his office, and she asks if they can have a cup of coffee. He hesitates because he thinks it is to talk about the two of them, but in fact that is not what she wants to talk about at all. She wants to talk about Loretta.

They go to the diner, where they sit in a corner booth and order. When their coffee arrives, Andrea asks, "Can you tell me something about the boy?"

"I haven't heard much in a while. He got into some trouble a few years back. And there was something about drugs. I think he's actually a bit of a con artist. I've heard stories about him calling Loretta and Patrick, saying that someone's threatening to kill him . . . making up stories about not having money. Bilking them, really. They haven't seen him in years."

"Did he go to school? Didn't he grow up here?"

"They sent him to all these fancy schools. He was thrown out of several. Then I think he told them he was going to business school at NYU. They sent him money to cover his tuition, paid his bills. But he wasn't even enrolled. I think the last straw was some strange thing about Las Vegas. He called and said he'd lost his wallet. He needed money. They wired him money on a Visa card, and he used the card number to run up a lot of debt. There was something about a huge sum in cash advances. Anyway, I think they do what they have to, to keep him alive. Or to keep him out of a scandal. It seems as if they're always putting out fires. Basically, as far as I can tell, they've given up on him."

Andrea says, "I thought perhaps there was some hope."

Gil shakes his head. "It's a pretty closed case, as far as I can tell.

In all the years I've known Loretta, I've rarely heard her mention him."

Andrea nods. "She's never mentioned him to me."

Then Gil gazes around the diner, and when he sees no one is looking, he reaches across the table to touch her hands. "But what about us, Andrea? I miss you. I haven't seen you in a while."

"I thought you didn't want to talk about us." He looks down. Andrea feels the warmth and roughness of his hands. She tries to remember his touch, but it is as if the affair happened long ago, to someone else. She misses him, too, but in a vague, undetermined way. With Charlie it was the specifics she missed—his "touch base" phone calls, his shoulder, his sleeping body. The habit of him. But with Gil there was no habit. It was the immediacy she longed for, where she could lose herself. Now she no longer wants that.

She is at the place she has come to before in relationships, when the person looks the way he did when she first met him, before any specialness was attributed to him. Gil has come full circle. She sees him once again as a rather stiff, middle-aged man in a tweed jacket and Burberry raincoat, like a character in a tawdry French film. "I don't think I can . . ." she tells him, rubbing her fingers over his hands. How can she tell him? *I am in another place. I have moved on to other things.*

She lets him go and his hands drift back across the table into his lap. She puts a dollar down for her coffee. He tries to give it back to her. "It's okay, Gil," she says, and, stuffing the dollar under her saucer, she walks away.

Six

In early December the temperature soars into the fifties and low sixties. The pond thaws and the dogs enjoy swimming in it again. It begins to rain, a slow steady rain. Then the wind shifts, and a cold Arctic wind comes down from Canada. There is a sudden freeze. Still Andrea takes her dogs and heads out.

She needs mittens. A scarf. She wears her hiking boots with the cleats. Her dogs slip as they race ahead. When she comes to the pond, she sees a duck struggling in the center. It is flapping, and at first Andrea thinks it has broken a wing. But then she sees its orange webbed foot, trapped in the ice. The duck must have fallen asleep in the water and then awakened, surprised by the freeze.

The duck is flapping, trying to pull its webbed foot free. It squawks, spins on its leg. Chief is racing across the glazed surface of the pond after the duck. "Come here, Chief," Andrea calls as the duck honks in distress.

But Chief is after it. Andrea steps out on the pond, just a few yards. She feels the pond give, cracking slightly under her feet. The duck tugs more frantically as Chief slides along the ice. "Chief," Andrea calls.

The dog continues, his front paws extended, and the frantic duck tries to fly until suddenly Andrea hears an odd ripping sound, then a crack. There is a furious flutter of wings as the duck breaks free, leaving its webbed foot behind.

"You know," Barbara says, "I never trusted her."

Andrea sits in her mother's breakfast nook as Barbara, her thick black hair, now streaked with gray and tumbling down her shoulders, tries to scramble eggs and make toast. "Who?" Andrea asks. She is wearing the aqua turtleneck Loretta gave her, and it is irritating her around the neck. She scratches at a reddish welt. It must not be pure cashmere. Her mind has wandered to the organic canola oil, no-salt eggs her mother is stirring, which she knows will be tasteless. The five-grain toast is burning.

"Elena, of course. Damn it . . ." Barbara plucks the burned toast from the toaster and swats away the smoke so the smoke alarm won't go off. She tosses the toast in the garbage and puts in two more pieces. "There was always something about her."

"It's just hindsight, Mom. When she and Dad were together, they seemed fine. You hardly gave her a thought." Andrea is restless, and she is also hungry. It takes her mother so long to put food on the table. Andrea has come over in part for a holiday brunch and in part to borrow money, which is often her reason for coming to see her mother.

"Not exactly. I had a feeling about her. You could never get a straight answer out of her." Barbara reaches into a pocket and removes a clip. She grabs her hair and pulls it back. Gray strands still fall around her face, and she keeps pushing them away.

Andrea rises when she sees smoke coming from the toaster again. "Let me help you, Mom."

"No, no, I just want you to sit and talk to me. We never get to do that."

"I can help and talk at the same time." But she sits back down. "What do you want me to talk about?"

Barbara heaves a sigh. These mundane tasks—making breakfast, chatting with her daughter—are too much for her. She is better in a lab, drawing on a pipette, checking her stem-cell research. Here her incompetence is all too obvious. She is a large woman, imposing, a heavier version of her daughter, with the same disheveled look. Her beige wool slacks are stained, and there's a tear under the arm of her blouse. Barbara says, "You know, talk about whatever daughters talk to their mothers about . . . It's not every day I get to fix you breakfast."

Andrea almost quips back, "Thank God," but catches herself. "No, it's not," she says.

The TV is on mute, but CNN is on, and its ticker tape keeps going around. Experts are advising people to stock up on bottled water and batteries. People are emptying their bank accounts. There is concern about terrorist activity on New Year's Eve. Andrea can't take her eyes off it. Something awful has happened to a school-child in England. A head coach somewhere has resigned. Doom and horror are mixed with birthday greetings.

Andrea picks up the remote and switches to a speechless talk show. The audience gives a silent shriek. "You know, Mom, I just think we all got it wrong. But how could Dad have made such a mistake?"

Barbara gives her an ironic look. "Darling, you forget, your father was a very complicated man. He made his own choices, and they weren't always the right ones. He was blind to certain things. His own mother, for example."

"My grandmother—"

"She was a very cold person."

"Yes, but what happened to him?"

"Your father never had much self-knowledge. Elena was also a very cold person." Barbara puts a plate of runny eggs and burned toast in front of Andrea. "In some ways he brought it all on himself."

This plate of eggs and toast reminds Andrea of everything that is the matter with her life. It is like an affront. Aren't mothers supposed to know how to do these things? Isn't there some instinct that's supposed to take over? Andrea remembers once telling a guidance counselor that she wanted to search for her biological parents. The problem was, she told the counselor, she wasn't adopted.

"How did he bring that on? Tell me. How?" Andrea fiddles with the plastic horse-shaped clip she wears, rearranging her hair.

"He just did." Barbara pours herself a cup of coffee, spilling some into the saucer. She dumps in cream and sugar. Andrea notes that her mother's hand is trembling as she sits down. "So tell me about your friendship with Loretta. What's it like having such a famous friend?"

Andrea shrugs. "I don't think of her as famous. Not really." She takes a bite of eggs. They are tasteless and she wants to ask for salt, but she knows there will be another sigh, a heaving. Besides, she is happy to talk about Loretta. "Loretta has taken a real interest in me. I don't know how to explain this, but she's like, well . . ." Andrea hesitates over the words that are on the tip of her tongue— "a mother to me"—but she doesn't say that. Instead she says, "She's like family to me. You know, we go back and forth between our houses all the time. We share books. I go over there for dinner, for drinks, a lot."

"That's good," Barbara says, smiling. She seems genuinely pleased for her daughter. "It's nice that you have a person like that in your life. An older person."

"Yes, we share a lot. She bought a painting from me." Even as Andrea says it, she wishes she hadn't.

"She did? That was very nice of her."

Already Andrea is annoyed with herself for telling her mother. "She didn't do it to be nice."

"Oh no, of course not." Barbara puts her hand to her mouth.

"She paid a thousand dollars. She just wrote out a check." Andrea realizes after she says this that it will be difficult now to borrow money from her mother. Beyond this Andrea feels a twinge. It still bothers her that the painting was not on the wall for Patrick's birthday. Or at least given to him in some formal manner.

She remembers how empty she felt, wandering through the various arms of the house, sneaking as she looked for it. It was as if she gave this woman a piece of her heart, and it was nowhere to be found. But now the painting is on the wall where people can see it. In her mind Andrea can see the picture hanging above Patrick's desk.

"Which painting?" Barbara asks.

Andrea forgot that her mother has never seen this series. "It's actually a painting of our house on Shallow Lake. I've been doing a series."

Barbara nods and takes a sip of her coffee. "I know. Robby told me. I'd like to see this work sometime, but honey, you know you are a wonderful girl. A beautiful girl. I just want you to be happy in this life."

"And . . ." Andrea draws the word out, waiting for what her mother will say next.

"Its time to move on. Get past all of this. Elena, the house, you know, the whole thing."

"God," Andrea says, "that's what everyone tells me. I *am* getting on with my life. And my work is my own business, just like yours."

"Of course it is. I only mean that it would be good for you to put your father and all of this behind you." Barbara sighs, staring at Andrea's half-eaten breakfast.

"Anyway, Loretta is helping me. She's interested in me and my work." Andrea pushes her plate away. "She's my friend."

Loretta has invited Andrea not only for her annual tree trimming, which is always held the Saturday before Christmas and is a kind of open house with all the "usual suspects," but also for Christmas Day, which is a more intimate affair. Andrea has never truly celebrated the holidays. "I was raised by atheists. Basically I'm a pagan," she likes to say. But she enjoys the idea of going to Loretta's for Christmas dinner. "It will be small," Loretta has promised. "Just a few close friends."

Though Andrea never gets gifts for her mother or Robby, she

wants to get the Partlows something. She has only sixty dollars in her bank account until the end of the month. So with the hundred dollars Barbara slipped into her hand as she was leaving ("To buy yourself something nice"), Andrea goes to the mall, fighting her way through the crowds. She stops in at Bookends, but she decides a book would just be coals to Newcastle.

She goes from store to store until she comes to a little tucked-away gardening shop, where she looks at bulbs and seed packages, all of which she rejects. A nice planter doesn't seem quite right for Loretta. Then Andrea lands on a yellow watering can. It is bright and cheerful. Then she goes to the liquor store and gets Patrick a good bottle of single-malt Scotch.

On Christmas afternoon Andrea makes her way toward the Partlows', her gifts in a sack. It is snowy and slippery. Her cheeks are cold, and she feels like a character in a Victorian novel. Smoke is coming from Loretta's chimney. Andrea walks quickly toward the warm house.

Inside, a blaze of lights and a roaring fire greet her. The Three Tenors singing "Adeste Fidcles" comes from all directions. The tree, which stands in the middle of the living room, is tall and decorated with white lights and candles. It has ornaments from all over the world—a glass panda from China, an Eiffel Tower, a woven camel from Egypt, assorted painted balls from Russia, African musical instruments.

"We always make a point of bringing an ornament home," Andrea hears Patrick explaining to no one in particular. The guests who have already arrived stand around the tree. "And our friends bring us ornaments from around the world." It is indeed a small gathering. Jim Adler and his wife, Loretta and Patrick, the Vitales from across the way, and Arnie Wexler, a remote, craggy-faced man and professor of medieval history.

Andrea is greeted by the smells of goose and cranberries, mulled wine. Patrick's buttery fruit pies stand cooling on a sideboard. He takes Andrea's coat and her gifts. "You shouldn't have."

"Oh, I wanted to, please don't think anything of it."

He unwraps the Scotch, which cost her almost fifty dollars, "Andrea, this is so generous of you, so kind."

Loretta seems genuinely thrilled with her watering can. She holds it up, tips it so she can see how it would pour. "It's charming. I just love it. I'll always be thinking of you when I'm watering my plants." Putting the can down, Loretta takes Andrea aside. "I have something for you," she says. She takes Andrea by the arm and ushers her along one of the corridors, a wing Andrea doesn't think she's been down before. Past a guest room into the den with a large TV. It is a dark-wood, cozy room, lined, of course, with books. On the table sits a narrow package wrapped in silver paper. Loretta reaches for it. "Open it," she says.

Andrea cradles the package in her hand. There is a tiny card and she reads it. "Dear Andrea: for your wonderful work, fondest wishes for the year ahead, Loretta." Andrea smiles and thanks her for the card. She slips the gift out of the silver paper. It is in a long, slender box covered in a silk brocade.

Andrea opens the box and finds five sable brushes—there are a fine point, a fan, two medium points, and a large brush. Andrea lifts the large brush out of the box, runs her fingers over its bristles. "These are just beautiful."

"I want you to paint something wonderful with them," Loretta says with a smile. Andrea hugs her. "You must show me when you have. Now put them away. I don't want the others to see."

It is time for dinner. Jim is going to carve. The goose, brown, overflowing with chestnut stuffing, is brought in on a platter, and everyone applauds. Andrea helps with the spinach souffle, the yams. There is onion marmalade, a cranberry ring. As Andrea holds plates, Jim loads them with goose and trimmings. "It is so nice to see you here," Jim says. He seems genuinely pleased. "And to see one of your paintings on the wall!"

Andrea is thrilled that he noticed. "Yes, she bought it for Patrick's birthday."

"It is very good to see you finding a place for yourself here."

Over dinner they chat about school, about holidays, about politics. Andrea comes back with quick jibes, a joke about the provost that everyone finds funny. Afterward Loretta says, "Now, I know this is hokey, but Arnie plays the piano, and we like to sing carols. Would you all mind? It is our little tradition over the holidays."

It does seem rather hokey, but then Andrea thinks, Why not? She stands by the piano. The fire blazes and she is warm. She shares a song sheet with Patrick as they sing "Joy to the World." She opens her mouth and sings. She is surprised at the sound of her own voice, so deep and resonant. It is as if she has never sung before.

She wakes up the next day with an urgent need to paint. She wants to use the sable brushes and see what they can do. But a million things get in her way. The heat isn't working, and the Romanellis ask her to help them check the pilot light. Then Robby calls to say he had a horrible Christmas and that he's thinking of leaving Marty. It isn't until late in the day that Andrea packs her book bag, slipping the brocade box into a pouch. Then it takes the car almost half an hour to warm up. Finally, when it is really dark, she drives to the visual arts building.

All the way over she thinks about the brushes. How she can't wait to use them. She is lost in thought, thinking about what she might paint. She sees a kind of Romare Bearden landscape, almost collage-like, as she locks her car and walks toward Rinkley. She is about to put her key in the door when someone grabs her from behind. She feels the hands across her face as she is dragged toward some bushes.

She knows she should let go of her bag. Whoever it is will be wanting her purse and what is in it. Andrea doesn't mind giving up her wallet, her meager cash, but she will lose the brushes. And that is not possible. With all her strength, she struggles. She screams even as a hand goes over her mouth. As she feels the hand clamp down, she bites, digs her teeth in hard, breaking flesh. As her attacker pulls away, she leaps in the air and with all her might jabs her elbows and feet into his sides. She hears a deep moan and sees him crumple to the ground.

Turning, Andrea sees Gil Marken rubbing his shin, gazing at his hand. She is trembling with fear and rage. "I can't believe you did this, you asshole."

"Boy, I guess I don't have to worry about you."

"What did you do? Follow me here?"

"No, I saw you drive by."

Her bag has fallen, and the brushes have tumbled out into the snow. Quickly she snatches them up. "There's something the matter with you," she says.

"It's just a joke. Can't you take a joke?"

When Gil reaches for her, she shoves him away. "Get out of here," she says. "I must have been crazy—" She turns and goes inside, not finishing her thought.

She is still shaking when she gets upstairs. How could she have been so stupid? Before, this might have turned her on. Aroused her. But now everything is so clear. It is as if she never saw things for what they were. She turns on the lights, walks around her studio, this little room that has become the focus of all she does. Slipping out of her jeans and sweater, she puts on her paint clothes. Loose-fitting and comfortable.

She wants a drink. Something to calm her nerves. There's some red wine left from the last time Gil was over, but she resists pouring herself a glass. She thinks, he's just an idiot. Then focuses her attention on the wall before her. She takes the sable brushes and puts them on her bench. She sets up a canvas. She has some ideas, nothing specific, but she wants to paint.

She starts with blue, a brighter color than she's used in a while. She begins with the medium-size brush. It is odd, because it has been a gray wintry day, yet she paints the house in summer, surrounded by delphinium and roses, an imprecision of color and form. Slowly a man who could be a father and a little girl take shape, sitting on the porch.

She paints the sweep of the house. The expanse of lawn.

As she paints, she thinks about this vista that exists only from the center of Shallow Lake. She is in the boat that day, fishing. All four of them are there. There is fried chicken, juicy and crisp. The sun is blazing, and it is a stunning day. Her mother is looking up, tears in her eyes. "Why do you always have to be right? Why do you have to be like this?"

"Because I do," her father says. And then, "Because I am." There is something final, almost frightening, in his voice.

He is not a man to cross.

Barbara has forgotten something—the salt, drinks. Andrea can't recall what. "How could you be so stupid? Why is it so difficult to pack a picnic?" her father demands. The sky has turned cloudy, and it is cold in the boat. Andrea huddles in the back, making herself small, not wanting to be seen. And then calmly, smiling, not just to Barbara but to all of them, he says, "If there's a wrong way to do something, you'll find it, won't you?"

Andrea is inside the boat, painting what she sees.

She pauses, stepping back from her canvas. Why is it that she can never see the house after she turned ten? Why does it seem frozen in time? Putting her brush down, Andrea walks to the window. Moonlight comes in. She gazes down at the campus—the long stretches of green, the walkways.

Then she looks back at all the paintings, these strange miniature canvases of a house in all its stages of repair and decay, with dolls torn apart, shadows she cannot explain, as if a monster looms over them.

Andrea understands that the house is frozen in time. There were whole years, a decade, when she never went there. The years she has forgotten. She was never invited. Never allowed. Andrea sits down on the floor in front of her work, dropping her head in her hands. How is this possible? she asks herself. And why am I remembering it now?

————

Her father skates with her. He is a graceful skater with an even glide. As they skate, he counts. "One two three four, crossover, one two three four, progressive, leg roll, sashay." She feels the firmness of his one hand on her back, his other guiding her across the ice.

If she loses count, if she skips a step, he bites his lips and shakes his head. "Let's start again," he says. "You can count, can't you?" And later, when she is very good, when she and Robby skate together and they spin or he lifts her off the ice and they have almost perfected their act, there is always their father at rinkside, shaking his head.

"You know what your problem is?" Robby tells her when she says she wants to give up skating. "You let him get to you."

But Andrea protests. "I want something that's mine," she says. "Something he can't take away."

All through the winter break Andrea paints. It is as if the sable brushes can do nothing wrong. Andrea does not want to stop. She loses track of the days, of time. She has never worked like this before. New images come to her powerfully, like pyrotechnics, and she is afraid if she stops, they will as well. She is painting even on New Year's Eve, when her cell phone rings.

"Andrea," Loretta says, "what are you doing? Now, get yourself over here and usher in the millennium. We need to see if the world is going to come to an end. Patrick and I have a bet riding on it."

When Andrea arrives, a small group has gathered—mostly

neighbors, a few faculty members from the writing program. The TV is on, and the ball is about to drop on the New Year, the new decade, the new century, the next thousand years. In Paris the New Year is ushered in without a hitch. They all gaze at Paris, its lights shimmering as always. The City of Lights. Andrea feels as if everything is before her.

Just as the ball drops, Patrick uncorks the champagne with a loud pop. He is still expecting the world to end, and it is only moments away.

And then it happens. The year, the decade, the millennium switch over and the lights stay on. Water flows from the pipes. No planes tumble out of the skies. "I told you," Loretta says, beaming, raising her glass, "nothing would happen. It's going to be a very good year."

Glasses clink in the air. They all wish one another the best of everything. Andrea hugs Loretta and Patrick. Then she drives back to her studio and paints with her sable brushes until dawn.

Her students sit, staring at Andrea, as she talks about the light. "Your job as artists," she tells them, "is finding the light in the painting." The artists she admires are the ones who make it seem as if the light is coming out of the painting. Rembrandt, Turner, Redon, Dorman.

She shows them a slide of the work of Albert Pinkham Ryder, and they listen as she describes how he spit tobacco on his paintings, baked them in the oven, rubbed dirt and cigar ashes on them, all in order to give them their eerie, melancholy mood. But now these paintings are falling off the canvas. They are in ruins.

"Still," Andrea tells the students, "I have to admire the effort. I like his spontaneity. In my own work I never think of ideas. Often I don't know before or after what I've done."

Marc gives her a questioning look. "I don't understand," he says.

"Matisse said that when we grow up, we must learn to be children again. I try to paint like a child. I try not to think about what I'm doing or why."

When had the trouble begun? When she was eleven or twelve. Or even earlier. And then, of course, she was the trouble. She had "acted out," as her therapists said. Been disruptive in school, run away many times. There had been boys and drugs. An odd mix of things. They'd found her in alleyways, drunk, even as a young teenager. Some nights she didn't come home.

Barbara had been beside herself, while her father had been quite clear. Andrea was invited to the lake house, only if she behaved. But she didn't behave. At first it was just mischief. Smashing the lawn gnomes: Robby put her up to it. But then it was more serious. She stole things. Money from Elena's wallet. She had people over, questionable people, older boys who drove, and drank when her father and Elena were out. Which was most of the time when she went to stay with them. She argued with her father. "Why do you make us come here if you're not going to be around?"

After one more incident involving the police and a neighbor's complaint about noisy parties and drinking, her father put his foot down. She was no longer welcome at Shallow Lake. He would see her at his house in Montrose. He would take her to dinner, but she could not come up to the lake house.

And she had never gone again.

He phoned her once a week, but often Andrea would not take his calls. They did not speak for months, years, at a time. Just like Robby said. But she would call when she needed him. And she did. She called to cry into the phone, to beg him to come and get her. Once she called from a phone booth in the middle of nowhere. And he came. He always did. He could never say no. Not when she pleaded with him like that.

There were the late-night calls from street corners and phone booths, the calls from New York when she'd run out of money. The cries for help. She'd run away and Barbara couldn't find her. The few times she'd had encounters with the law, when men left her high and dry, when she had nowhere to turn, he had been there. All she had to do was call.

Simon Geller had a weakness for his daughter. Perhaps because he had left her; he'd let himself be pulled away. And he felt guilty. She knew this. It was a certain power—a small one, perhaps, but a power nonetheless—she exerted over her father. She knew: when she needed him, he would come. And now he was gone.

He had, of course, been gone for years, but the finality of it strikes her once again.

From her apartment Andrea can see into the Partlows' living room and sometimes she sees Loretta, standing at the window, staring out. She imagines that Loretta is thinking about her next book— about the characters and the world they will inhabit. She also understands something she has not understood before. Loretta wants another chance. A fresh start. It's normal that people would want this in this world. A chance of making things good.

Andrea cannot explain it, but she has felt a change in herself since she started spending time with Loretta. She has become aware of the softness of flannel against her skin, how sleep makes her happy. One morning she woke up laughing. She savors the taste of oranges on her lips. She smells a freshness in the air that didn't seem to be there before. On cold days she finds herself making soup.

It is as if the world is not so dark, as if a burden has been lifted. As if this was what she needed, and all she needed. To tell her story. Over and over again. It has freed her up. She feels lighter than she has in years. On the door of her office she posts an appointment schedule, and students come to see her. They sit in a chair across from her and talk about an idea they have for a drawing, a painting, a film. They share with her their hopes and dreams. What they want to be when they grow up.

One afternoon Marc appears. He brings a set of sketches he has done, based on an assignment she gave them: draw faces from memory. He has drawn a series of self-portraits as a small child, though from before he could have had a sense of himself. But the expression is that of an older person. "I like the layers of time in this piece," Andrea says to him. "It is a child who isn't a child."

She looks forward to class now. Her students listen to her, watch her. She thinks how alone each of them is—away from family and home. How they have been entrusted to her. It is a precious gift, really. She sees them in process, innocent and unformed, the way she was before all of this happened in her life.

She can make a difference in their lives. It never occurred to her before. She has made a point to learn their names. When they come to her office, she asks them about themselves.

She walks around studio class, pausing at Beth's easel. Beth has blue hair and a grim expression, as if something is always going wrong. "It's good," Andrea tells her, and Beth steps back from the work. She sees it as Andrea does. Then Beth's face opens like a flower.

A few days later, Andrea is invited to Loretta's for tea. More and more she has come to rely on these afternoon teas when the table is set. Fine china, homemade oatmeal and gingerbread cookies (Patrick bakes them) on a tray. Andrea looks forward to these meetings that happen so easily ("Hello, dear, we saw your light on. Are you free for a drink?") that she has almost forgotten why she arranged them in the first place.

At each visit Loretta plies Andrea with books and magazines, things she must read, must see. She must know about an archaeological site in Cambodia, the truth about Lewis and Clark, the fascinating story of a mother and daughter separated during the Holocaust and reunited through a bizarre coincidence in a hospital. Endless stories, tales, works of famous painters. "We just saw the van Gogh show. It's too bad it's his madness that's remembered. There was so much more to him than that. I can't believe the vitality of that man."

Andrea takes home the books and devours them. She stays up late, as if cramming for an important exam, reading everything Loretta passes on to her. She goes to the studio, and her painting improves. Her canvases grow larger, and to her surprise, she stops painting the house.

Or rather, she stops painting it in the same way. The house grows smaller, more remote. It is no longer the central image. It is off to the side, in the background. No longer the focal point. Soon, Andrea knows, it will go away.

There is brightness in the paintings now. Color. The shapes grow abstract, lopsided. She scribbles on paper, paints on top of it. Her work is no longer recognizable, even to her. It is as if a different person is working inside her. She believes all this change comes from the sable brushes Loretta gave her. Every night when she is done, she cleans and dries the brushes, then sets them on a cloth for the next day.

At night Andrea sleeps in a way she hasn't in years. The dark circles that hung like small boats under her eyes have receded. She takes long, relaxing baths in eucalyptus gel and scrubs her skin with lemony soap. Her hair is rich and textured once more, and her eyes have a clarity to them. Their redness is gone. People who haven't seen her in a while say Andrea seems to sparkle.

They say she looks like someone who has been on a long vacation, a cruise, when in fact she's never left home.

She is working blindly one afternoon, in the frenzy that has been coming over her more and more lately, when someone knocks. The knock startles her. Rarely does anyone show up here. She assumes it is Garcia, the security guard, checking on her, but when she opens the door, she sees Jim Adler. He is grinning through his thick gray beard.

"Andrea. I thought I'd find you here. Am I disturbing you?"

"Oh, no," Andrea says, though of course he is. She shakes her head as if she is waking. Like some head-injury victim, she tries to remember where she is, what day it is. Anyone other than Jim she would turn away. She wipes her hands on her jeans. "Come in."

Slowly, still smiling, he enters her studio. He gazes around, takes in her new work. "Yes, Loretta said it was very interesting, this house series. It's a kind of compulsion, isn't it?"

Andrea cocks her head, put off by this comment. "I prefer to think of it as an obsession. An artistic obsession, at that."

"Yes, perhaps that is better," he says. "Well, it is an interesting series. You do seem to be going deeper. Do you still have a gallery?"

"Not really." Andrea hasn't been in touch with her old gallery in years.

"I'll mention it to my dealer."

"Thank you," Andrea says, grateful.

Then Jim Adler sits down on her stained and splattered sofa. He pats the place beside him and she joins him there. "You know, Andrea, I've always liked you. I've always admired your work. You haven't had an easy time, and so I have tried to be a friend. I hope I have."

"Yes, you have. Definitely."

"That's why I came here today. Because I do care about you."

Andrea nods. "I appreciate that, Jim."

His face turns serious. "There are some things you should be aware of." He leans toward her, then away, as if he cannot find a comfortable spot. "I think you should know that some people are talking about you."

"About me?" she says with a laugh. "Why? I can't believe they'd waste their breath."

"Well, they are. I'm not sure what it is. They know about you and Gil. I think even Lila knows."

Andrea's eyes widen. "They do? But that's been over—"

"It's very threatening to some of the marriages, to some people in this town."

"Jim, I'm not even seeing him anymore. I hardly speak to him. I think he's kind of crazy." She gets up, finding it difficult to catch her breath. "I don't understand. Who is saying these things?"

"It doesn't matter. You know how people are."

Andrea shakes her head in disbelief. "I don't know what to say. I find this very strange."

"Well"—he pats her leg—"perhaps people are jealous. It is a small town. A lot of people would love to be at Loretta Partlow's every chance they get. You know, people can be very petty. Anyway, your review is in the spring, and I just think you need to know some of these things. Perhaps you can correct them. Maybe be a little more friendly."

"I'm not seeing Gil any longer, and I see no reason why my friendship with Loretta should bother anyone."

"Look, I just want to protect you."

"I appreciate that, but I'm not sure I'm someone to envy."

"I know you've had a hard time. That's why I thought I should say something." He drops his head. "One other thing. Some of your students have complained. It isn't very serious, but they say you have been missing appointments with them. That you are always late. I've heard some reports."

Andrea nods. She thinks of that hostile message from Greg. "Perhaps I have been late and missed a few appointments. But I am working on that. I do want to do better in this regard. I think I'm doing a good job."

Jim Adler stands up, ready to leave. "I'm glad to hear that." He heads to the door. "I want things to go well for you here." He kisses her lightly on the cheek. "And I do like this new work. It has an energy to it. You seem very invested in it."

Andrea stares at Jim as he leaves. He doesn't really know her now. She is a different person from the one she was a few months ago. The people in Hartwood haven't caught up to her yet. That's all.

Shaking her head, she picks up her brushes and tries to begin where she left off. But she cannot get back into the groove. She paints until she is tired, though never quite concentrating. Then she glances at the clock. It is almost four, and it is a day for high tea. Andrea realizes she did not confirm, but she is sure Natalie and Patty will be there.

Andrea gets in her car and races to the faculty hall, where the teacups and plates are already being carted away. Only a few people remain in the room. In the leather chairs she sees Natalie sitting with Loretta. Loretta, dressed in a navy pantsuit, her hair pulled back, is slumped in a big green chair, looking very relaxed. Natalie gives her a wave. "Patty couldn't make it," Natalie says, "but I ran into Loretta here."

"Hello, dear," Loretta says, taking Andrea's hand. She is wearing a pinkish lipstick, and when Andrea bends over, Loretta's lips just brush her cheek. "Oh yes, we heard Natalie's chamber orchestra in the city this weekend. I was just telling her."

Natalie blushes, folding her long legs and arms into one another. "You should have let me know you were going."

"It was a last-minute thing. We were already in the city. I saw that the Mozart Ensemble was playing."

Andrea has her tea and the few picked over sandwiches that remain. The tea is tepid. She is surprised Loretta would catch a concert in town at the last minute. Loretta hardly ever goes into the city and hardly ever does anything like that on the spur of the moment. Andrea is still upset about her visit from Jim Adler and is also trying to remember when Natalie told Loretta the name of the group she played with.

Loretta goes on, "It was very good. Especially the modern music. I was surprised you don't just do Mozart. But you played the Harbison concerto beautifully."

"It is a difficult piece," Natalie says, "but I love playing it."

"I always like to follow the work of our junior faculty. So," Loretta gets up, "I should get going. I've got lots to do. I'll see you in the next day or so, right, Andrea?"

Andrea nods, smiling. "I'll bring those books by."

"There's no rush." Loretta leaves, moving quickly, slinging her bag over her shoulder. Andrea thinks that she looks like a young woman from behind.

That night, thinking over her conversation with Jim Adler, Andrea wonders if people really are talking about her in this way. Why would Jim Adler say something if it weren't true? She calls Charlie but gets his machine. She feels like she has to speak with someone. If people are talking about her, Loretta would know. Though it is later than she'd like, after nine, she can see Loretta working at her computer, so she calls.

"I'm sorry to bother you," Andrea says.

"It's all right. I was just reading."

Andrea pauses, because she knows this isn't the truth. Why would Loretta say she was reading if she was writing? Why would she need to lie to Andrea? Perhaps she was reading online. That makes sense, and Andrea, who realizes she is feeling slightly paranoid, goes on. "I was wondering. I know this is a little strange. But Jim Adler told me that people were talking about me . . . I'm not sure what it's about. They think, well, I'm not sure what they think. I was just wondering . . ."

"What, dear?"

This is a stupid conversation, Andrea thinks. "If you've heard anything. Has anyone said anything about me to you?"

There is quiet on the other end of the line. "No, dear. Not at all. Why would anyone do such a thing? But if they do, if I hear anything, I'll be sure and let you know."

"Thank you, Loretta. I thought you would."

Andrea stays up late so she can read the new books Loretta has lent her. She wants to return them so she can borrow more. It is not exactly that she wants more books to read or more to do, but she has this link, this ongoing connection, with Loretta. She has to keep it alive. A kind of hunger has come over her that she cannot explain. She feels as if she cannot stop. As if she has to keep going.

Because she has become so restless, she takes longer walks with her dogs, sometimes late at night. As she walks, she thinks about all that has been happening in her life. Her bond with Loretta, which, despite Andrea's original impetus, seems to be deepening. Her loss of interest in Gil. The changes in her work.

Though Andrea remains bothered by Jim Adler's visit, she knows it has to do with a person she was, not who she is now. Eventually this will be clear to everyone! It is as if her life has been a series of unwoven threads, and they are coming together into a pattern, a tapestry shaping itself into a recognizable whole.

Even her work has taken on a new dimension. She has begun painting out of the box, beyond the frame, filling a canvas, letting it spill over the edges. Already she is beginning to think of what she'll do next. It is as if her own self is spilling onto the floor, and she has no desire to stop it.

As she walks late at night, she makes a loop around the neighborhood. She takes the path out to the pond. It is still winter and the chill remains in the air. She wanders in the darkness, with only one light—a guiding light—burning in Loretta's studio.

One night, leaving the library late, Andrea runs into Charlie. She has an armful of slides and books, a book bag slung over her shoulder. She recognizes his easy lope. "Hey," she says.

"Need a hand?" Charlie asks. He is dressed in a suit, an overcoat, and his dark curls rustle in the wind.

"Sure," she says, and drops some books and a carousel of slides into his arms. He walks her to her car. "You look like you are coming from somewhere," she says.

"There was a concert. String quartet."

Andrea nods. She'd seen the posters. She'd meant to go. "How was it?"

"It was good," he says. "It's part of my job, you know. What I have to do." He sighs as they reach her car. "It was restful." She is glad he is alone. Glad she hasn't run into him with a date. After she unlocks the car, he drops the slides and books on the backseat. Andrea throws her book bag in.

"Would you like to go get a drink somewhere?" she asks tentatively, afraid he'll say no. "I mean, I know it's late . . ."

"No, I'd like that. Where shall we go?"

As they are mulling over their few options, she remembers the dogs. "They need a walk first."

They take separate cars to her place. She drives ahead but can see him in her rearview mirror, his face thoughtful, gentle, his eyes on her. She pulls up in front of her place, racing out of her car. "I'll just be a sec," she says, dashing up the stairs and coming back with the dogs.

They leap all over Charlie, remembering him. It is a cool evening, and they let the dogs run free toward the woods. They walk slowly, trailing behind, so that the dogs stop to see if they are coming. Charlie reaches for Andrea's hand. It is a simple gesture, and Andrea thinks how comfortable it feels. Somewhere near the pond he kisses her. "I have missed you," he says.

Then she whistles for her dogs and they head home.

A few days later, on a clear winter's afternoon, Andrea goes to Loretta's for tea. She has just dropped in, as she often does, and sits in the living room leafing through their collection of art books while Loretta finishes her work.

Kippy is at Andrea's side, and she strokes his back. When

Loretta walks in, Andrea looks up from her book. Loretta stands in the doorway, her gray hair pulled back, a woman easily old enough to be her mother who has become her friend and along the way her confessor. It is as if Andrea cannot be absolved until she has told Loretta all.

Something in her life is shifting. It reminds her of arctic ice during a thaw, huge chunks breaking apart. There is movement. And there are things she needs to say. She helps Loretta carry out a tray—ginger tea with lemon, finger sandwiches of salmon and cream cheese, little poppyseed cakes.

Andrea settles into the couch that once seemed so deep, as if she could tumble endlessly into the earth. But now she knows the drop is not so far. There really is so little to fear. Andrea says, "You know, there are things I've never told you about my father and me. Things I suppose I've never told anyone."

Loretta, dressed in jeans and a blue sweatshirt—her work clothes, as she calls them—looks up. "What's that, my dear?" She sits on the other side of Kippy, and both women sit stroking the dog.

"Robby was right about what he said at Thanksgiving. For years, all through high school and into college, my father and I barely spoke. I know it's not what I told you. Not how I made it seem between my father and myself. But it's almost as if I forgot what really happened in my life until you and I began to talk about it."

Loretta seems surprised, startled even, as Andrea goes on. "Yes, we didn't speak. I hated him and I suppose he hated me. I hated him for leaving my mother, for marrying Elena. I felt he had betrayed us, and of course he had. I thought he was selfish and only cared for himself. He did neglect me, really."

Even as Andrea says this, she wonders, Is it right to be saying this? After all, Loretta has been accused of neglecting her own son, whose name never even comes up in conversation. Andrea thinks that Loretta's eyes are flitting to the glass table where the picture of her son sits. Andrea wants to stop, but the movement of their hands, both stroking the little white dog, makes her keep talking. And Loretta seems so eager to know. "He neglected you?" Loretta says, amazed.

"Yes, you know that hiatus, well, it was really . . ."

"A break?"

"Yes. It was a break. I forgot about this, or pushed it out of my mind, but for years he completely abandoned us. When they were first divorced, he had joint custody. We went from house to house, but afterward, when he married Elena, she pulled him away. And he left us with our mother, who was very confused. She could hardly keep it together. I couldn't stand it. I ran away. A lot. Many times. Once I wound up—lost."

"Lost?"

"I got into trouble."

"With . . ."

"Men, drugs, alcohol, the police, you name it."

"What happened?"

"From time to time I'd call him when I was in trouble, and he'd bail me out. He always came when I called, that was the big thing. When I needed him in that way, he could be there. He just couldn't be there, you know, in the ordinary ways."

"So you had to invent trouble."

Andrea looks down. This is the hardest thing for her to say. "Yes, I had to invent trouble so he would come around. So he would come and get me."

Loretta keeps stroking Kippy, and Andrea does, too. The two women sit, sinking into the sofa, their voices barely whispers. Andrea goes on. "Anyway, we finally reconciled, though it took a long time. I guess I called; he came over. But then he sat me down and we talked. And we kept talking. The last five years before the accident were wonderful. I had the father I'd never had before, but for years, yes, I suppose you could say, I despised him. I didn't care if he lived or died."

"And so those calls? When he had to come and get you?"

"Oh, yes, they stopped." Andrea pauses, looking down. "A long time ago."

When Andrea finishes, they sit in silence. Then Loretta reaches across the sofa to clasp Andrea's hand. Andrea is surprised by the touch of the thin, bony fingers—a cool, soft touch. Loretta says, "You know, I am glad you told me all of this. I feel as if I understand you much better than I did before. It must have been very hard on you."

"It was," Andrea says, "very hard. I'd forgotten whole period of my life. Like a blackout. I forgot the terror I felt. I forgot that I hated him. It's as if there was this abyss and I just fell into it. Until I was twelve, I adored my father. And then I did again after I was twenty. But there was this time—eight years or more—when we didn't speak. I'm not sure I ever saw him."

"But you reconciled. You patched it up."

"Yes, after college. We had a kind of powwow. I told him everything. He just sat and listened." Andrea thinks of that afternoon when she called her father and they met at a restaurant in Manhattan and for hours he listened to everything she said. Much as

Loretta listens to her now. "I'm not sure why I'm telling you all of this," she says.

"Well, I'm glad you did."

After a while Andrea pulls herself off the sofa. "Loretta, thanks for . . . for everything. I can't tell you how much it means to me."

She feels light-headed, as if she's had too much wine, though she hasn't drunk a thing. Then she kisses Loretta on the cheek and leaves.

In a few days Andrea is back at Loretta's, making a salad for an impromptu dinner. "Just us," Loretta said when she'd called half an hour before. Andrea had driven over to the butcher to pick up the steaks, then come to Loretta's. Now they stand side by side sipping wine. "You know," Andrea says, "there are things about my father I hadn't remembered. It's coming back to me now."

"Like what?" Loretta asks. She is slicing leeks into a pot of boiling water.

"He had these rules. If you played a game, it was to win. If you want to watch birds, you have to name them. If you start something, you finish it. Things had to be just so—always his way. There were pointless rules about table manners and how to put dishes in the dishwasher. How to eat your soup."

Loretta laughs. "How to eat your soup?"

"Oh yes, you wouldn't believe it. If the soup was hot, you made your spoon go front to back, but if it was cold . . ." Andrea stands in the kitchen demonstrating, then starts laughing as well. "I can't even get it right now."

"It sounds as if it's a lot to expect from a child," Loretta says. Not without regret, Andrea notes.

Andrea waits a moment to see if Loretta will say more. When she doesn't, Andrea goes on. "You know what he used to say: he'd say, 'If there's a wrong way to do something, you'll find it.' Then he'd laugh at his own joke. Except it was never very funny."

"He sounds as if he was a kind of perfectionist."

"Yes, but in a harsh way. Especially to Robby. He was hard on Robby. He made fun of him. But with me he just expected things—things I couldn't live up to. At least that's how I remember it now. I think I've been suffering from emotional amnesia all my life."

"Here, dear," Loretta says, "have some more wine."

Andrea realizes that she has come to depend on her talks with Loretta. Despite her original objective—that she wanted to get back at Elena, wanted Loretta to write the story of her father's death so that Andrea could send it to her stepmother with a note that said, "I know."—these talks have taken on a life of their own. They have become essential to Andrea's sense of well-being. What she did not realize was how much it means to her when Loretta sits straight up, eyes on her, and listens.

Where was it written? Andrea thinks. "Attention is the greatest form of generosity." Or words to that effect. Simone Weil. It feels to Andrea as they talk, as they chop vegetables for dinner, that she has what she's always wanted. She has a friend who will listen.

Her father pushed her; it's true. Andrea has begun thinking about this in earnest only lately. He wanted her to achieve. "Never stop trying," that was his motto. There was no point in doing anything for the sheer pleasure of it. Everything Simon did was designed to better himself.

Andrea was doomed from the start—to try and to fail. To soar and descend. Crash and burn. She couldn't just ice skate, she tells Loretta now, or play golf. "I had to have a coach. I had to take lessons. If I walked, it was because I had to go somewhere."

For years she skated competition singles. Once she was a runner-up junior New England champion. "Of course that didn't satisfy him." Until high school she and Robby skated pairs. "He was always at the side of the rink, shouting at us, at our coach. He made notes of all the things we did wrong, then he read them to us over dinner. We could never please him. We gave up trying. First my brother, then me."

"But you became an artist—and a good one."

"Thank you, perhaps I did, but only because he knew nothing about art. I painted and sketched. It was my own. He couldn't intrude there."

Andrea tells Loretta about the bleakness of her early years. The endless efforts to please, her father's leaving. The long list of addictions she doesn't like to think about—cigarettes and booze, low-level drugs and men. "I did a lot of things I shouldn't have done. It took me a long time to give things up. I guess I have an addictive personality."

"But you pulled yourself out."

"Yes, I painted. I found what I wanted to do."

Loretta nods. "I can't remember who wrote 'An artist's revenge is her work.' "

"Yes, it was like that, I guess." Though even as Andrea says it, she thinks this doesn't sound right. "Well, for me it was more my solace, but whatever it was, it saved me. I went into therapy for a while, gave up smoking, drugs. One at a time. My dad and I patched it up. It took a little while, but we did. Then I got the job at the college . . . Things were good, really." Andrea pauses. "Then my father had his accident."

Loretta, who is peeling potatoes, seems almost asleep when Andrea stops talking. As if waking, she says, "I'd like to see you skate."

"Skate? Why, I haven't in years."

"Isn't it like riding a bicycle? Once you learn . . ."

The pond in the woods is still frozen over. The dogs ran across it a few days before. Andrea tests it by walking into the center. She has dug her skates, a pair of tarnished whites with rusty blades, out of a box. She polishes them and scrubs the blades with Brillo. Sharpening will have to wait.

There is a log by the side of the pond and Andrea sits on it, shivering, as she laces up her skates. She is surprised that they fit so snugly. It has been years since she put them on. Loretta stands above, watching as Andrea does the tight cross-stitch lacing. Then Loretta gives Andrea a hand and helps her to her feet.

Andrea makes her way slowly to the edge of the pond. With one blade, she tries the ice. It is firm, though a bit bumpy, not as smooth as a rink. But it will do. She glides out on one blade, then eases onto the other. She skates around once or twice, aware of the bumps, trying to get a feel for the ice. Her legs are stiff and cold, and she thinks that she will fall.

Then she hears a kind of music in her head. A waltz. She can almost feel her brother's hand clasping her from behind. In her mind she begins her count. One two three, one two three. Her legs release, her arms swing at her sides as she slides, feeling the rhythm of her limbs, hearing the music.

She does a front crossover, then swivels and skates backward. The only sounds are the wind in the branches and her blades on the ice. A slick, cutting sound. She crosses to the center, does a Mohawk to backward position, then does circle after circle of back crossovers. She is only vaguely aware of Loretta, clapping her mittened hands at the pond's edge.

Andrea does her three-turns on all sides, front and back, in and-out. She does a little spin, then races to the edge of the pond, where she skates with an invisible partner at her side.

Then she breaks free. She glides across the pond. The swift sound of her blades cutting the ice. She does figure eights, moving backward, forward, arms flowing like wings as she performs two waltz jumps, surprised when she makes her landings, then skates fiercely into a spin in the center of the pond where she goes around and around.

Afterward Loretta invites her back to the house for hot chocolate. "It's Aztec chocolate," Loretta explains. "We got it on our last trip to Mexico. It's very good. Nice and rich."

"Yummy," Andrea says, rubbing her cold cheeks, her hands. They clomp back through the woods, their feet crunching across the snow. Andrea has her skates slung around her neck. Loretta's house feels warm and inviting. In the kitchen Loretta takes out a copper pot. She pours in creamy whole milk, big spoonfuls of chocolate, stirring slowly. Andrea watches the chocolate dissolve into a whirlpool of darkness. They sit down at the kitchen table, gazing out at the pond, the woods. "I haven't skated like that in a long time," Andrea says. "It felt wonderful."

"It seemed to all come back to you."

"Yes, that's the thing with skating. It comes back quickly, once you get your balance."

"Balance?"

"It's all about edges, skating. Little shifts of your weight." Andrea does a small twist with her hips and turns around.

"You're so graceful," Loretta says, sniffing the chocolatey steam.

"Thank you. I wouldn't have done it if you hadn't asked me to. I do love to skate . . . I never thought I'd say that again."

"Yes, well, it shows. You have a real gift."

"You know," Andrea says, "you've been so supportive about everything." Two cardinals perch at a bird feeder outside, and for a moment the two women stare at the red birds. "I feel badly that we always seem to talk about me," Andrea goes on, "I've been thinking about this . . ."

"Oh, but you're the one who's been through so much." Loretta still stares at the birds with her sharp blue eyes.

"Yes, and I've appreciated how much you've listened. But you've been through things, too . . ."

Loretta pulls her head back with a little snap as if a rubber band just let it go. "What do you mean?"

Andrea is feeling fresh from her skate. Her skin tingles from the cold as it hasn't in years. She is feeling braver, more expansive. It seems she can broach this subject now. "I'm just saying I've told you so much, but I've never really listened to you. I mean, we've never talked about . . . well, things in your life." Loretta looks as her as if she doesn't know what Andrea's talking about. "Like your son." When Loretta still doesn't say anything, Andrea says his name. "Sean."

Even as Andrea says it, she thinks she has done the wrong thing. Her mind scrambles, trying to recall if Loretta has ever mentioned the name of her son; Andrea is sure she hasn't. She sees Loretta pull away, the way she did the day when Mrs. Romanelli touched her sleeve. A jump back, like a cornered animal.

Andrea realizes she needs to do something, to recover the moment when they were sitting at a table, warming themselves over steaming hot chocolate. It seems to her she has just lost something, let something slide down the drain. "It's helped me to talk about my father, so I thought it might help you to talk about your life. But I don't want to pry. I mean, it's your business."

Loretta puts down her cup and stares at Andrea as if to say "Then don't." "My son isn't something I need to talk about," Loretta says. Then, staring at the clock, "My God, it's late. Time for me to make supper."

"Let me help you," Andrea offers. She is hoping Loretta will ask her to stay.

Loretta is already up, digging in the vegetable bin for lettuce, a tomato. Four small lamb chops, which she places in a dish, sprinkles with salt. "No, there's nothing to do, really."

"Then I'll get going," Andrea says. A moment later, her cup still half full, she leaves and heads home.

She does not hear from Loretta for a day or two. When she stops in to return some books, Patrick answers the door. He looks somewhat surprised to see her. "Oh, Andrea," he says, "Loretta is working. Was she expecting you?"

Andrea is startled by the question. For months now she's been dropping things off, popping in to say hello. "No, if she's busy, I was just going to leave these . . ."

"I'll give them to her."

Andrea's dogs are with her, and she is ready to walk in the woods when she realizes she has to pee. Too much coffee, she thinks. It is an urgent, pressing feeling, and she cannot seem to stop it. She could turn around and go home, but the dogs clearly want to be on their way. "Patrick, this is somewhat embarrassing . . . I was just heading into the woods, and I was wondering if—could I use your bathroom?"

Patrick smiles, charming in his red and black flannel shirt, his jeans, the smell of pipe tobacco on him. He invites her in, points the way. The bathroom is scrubbed white, smells clean and fresh, of lavender potpourri.

It is amazing to Andrea that this house is always so tidy, nothing ever out of place no matter when she shows up. She has never seen a dish in the sink. Hesitantly she uses the toilet. After washing her hands, she dries them on her jeans.

On her way out, she passes Patrick's office. The door is open, and she decides to look in at her painting. She gazes into the office and above his desk sees the old poster from the Frankfurt book fair. The poster fits perfectly into the gray lines that were on the wall. Her painting is nowhere to be seen.

Patrick catches a glimpse of her near his office and gives her a grin. "I think your dogs are ready to go," he says, and ushers Andrea out the front door.

Seven

It is a spring morning, one of the first nice days since the gray of winter, as Andrea heads out the door. Loretta has been away for a few weeks—"The Jerusalem book fair, my publisher is insisting that I go." Andrea offered to take care of Kippy and to pick up the mail, but Loretta said, "No, dear, you must be busy. I'm sure. Besides, we have our regular house sitter."

Now spring break is over, and Andrea in a rush, running late, is on her way back to class. Her students are lined up at their easels. The problem for the day is drawing negative space. Each is told to darken a sheet of paper, then draw with an eraser. Take away space, don't delineate it.

As Andrea watches her students, erasers in hand, she realizes it has been a while since she last heard from Loretta. They exchanged an e-mail or two before spring break, but they've seen each other only once, a few weeks ago, when they crossed paths in the woods. They were friendly, walking a ways together, though ooth were in a hurry to be home and promising to make a plan soon.

But then time went by and Andrea has been busy with her own life. She knows this is a good thing—that she has been busy. She has taken on some studio drawing students, and her own work has been moving in new directions. She has also begun seeing more and more of Charlie. It wasn't what either of them expected. "It just happened," she told Robby.

So she is busy, but she still thinks it is odd that she hasn't heard from Loretta. She wonders if they are back from the book fair, then that stopover in England to see the British publisher, wasn't that it? Surely Loretta must be back, because the break is over, and she has a graduate seminar.

She hasn't been answering her e-mail. That doesn't surprise Andrea, not really, because Loretta sometimes forgets, sometimes doesn't look at her mail for weeks at a time. And then, Loretta complains, there are literally hundreds of messages: "Everyone writing to me, asking me to do something." Andrea cannot imagine this. Hundreds of messages.

Over the dreary winter months Loretta was always so quick to get back, so fast to reply to any little message from Andrea. Sometimes Andrea would dash off a note and Loretta would seem to answer before it was sent. It was as if they were actually chatting, having a real conversation. Once they fired off so many quick replies that Andrea picked up the phone and said, "Maybe we should just chat."

Then there was spring break. Andrea and Charlie went away to Puerto Rico. They stayed in a funky hotel with sandy sheets and

sipped drinks with pink umbrellas in them. They swam
stingrays and danced the merengue. As they stood on a balco.
overlooking the sea, Hartwood seemed far away. When they
returned, they began seeing one another more. They made dinner
and watched TV. At night she lay beside him, watching him
breathe. She was transfixed by the steadiness, the reliability, of his
breath.

So Loretta had, to some extent, slipped Andrea's mind, the way
any friend might for a week or two when one is busy. And it felt
good to Andrea to be busy. There were so many things to catch up
on, the mail, e-mail, a small crisis at school that needed tending to,
a group show inviting her to submit work, and then another week
or so went by, before Andrea realized she hadn't heard from
Loretta in weeks. Or was it a month?

Then Andrea phoned, but got the machine. That seemed
strange. "I always pick up when I hear your voice," Loretta once
said. Andrea could see from her window that their cars were in
the driveway, the light was on in the study, so Loretta must be
home. But the shades were drawn and Andrea did not catch
glimpses of them at night inside, the way she normally would.
Maybe they were away, on tour in Europe somewhere. It would
make sense that she wouldn't answer her mail. The lights could
be on a timer.

But perhaps Loretta was working. Perhaps there was a big proj-
ect. A new novel. Loretta could be lost in her work, the way she
had once seemed dazed when Andrea interrupted her at the library.
As if she didn't even know where she was. This thought brought
some satisfaction to Andrea, though she missed Loretta.

This all seemed to make sense. But then one Saturday evening, a warm night of early spring, Andrea sees the cars. A dozen or so parked on the block, and the people, other faculty members (she recognizes the provost), walking up her street, heading to the Partlows' for cocktails (It is always cocktails at the Partlows'; never dinner; they don't do dinner except for very special occasions). And there is a graduate student in a white jacket, handing flutes of champagne to the guests as they arrive.

Andrea is surprised at how many cars arrive. Cars coming and going. People stopping in, on their way elsewhere. People standing on the patio. The clinking of glasses. Waiters serving cheese puffs on trays. Andrea stands at her window. She counts ten, fifteen cars. She cannot understand how she was not invited. This does not seem possible to her. She reasons that it is all writing and literature faculty. People Loretta "owes." Sometimes she has these kinds of gatherings—"obligations," she calls them. This must be one of those.

Then Andrea sees Jim Adler and that medieval history professor Loretta tried to fix Andrea up with once. She can't quite believe it. For the past year she has practically lived at Loretta's house and now she finds she wasn't invited at all.

Andrea stands, then sits at her window half the night, watching, as if this is a movie and she its transfixed viewer until the last car has gone away, and then she stays at the window, waiting until the Partlow house has gone dark. And it does, except for the light that stays on in Loretta's studio.

Andrea watches Loretta's shadow move in and out of the light. She is amazed at Loretta's stamina. How she can type away even into the night after a big party. Andrea is tempted to get up and walk to the end of the cul-de-sac and tap on the window. Loretta would be startled, but Andrea would give her a little wave. she'd say, "it's me."

On Tuesday Andrea needs some things at the store. When she opens the fridge, there is no milk, no juice. She has no cereal. No eggs. Nothing to munch on. It surprises her that she has let her supplies get so low. She drives out to the SuperSave, near the mall, and begins taking whatever she needs off the shelves. She also gets cookies and soda, steaks and a head of iceberg lettuce. As she puts these things in her cart, Andrea wonders whom she plans to cook for. Who will eat all this food?

It occurs to Andrea that she hasn't been taking very good care of herself. That she needs to do things differently. Perhaps she should have a small party. Have people over. She never entertains. When she took the job at Hartwood, Jim Adler told her to have parties. "Always reciprocate," he said. Perhaps that was why Loretta hadn't invited her that night. Perhaps Loretta was reciprocating. In her head Andrea is planning whom she will invite, how she will fix up her place for a small party.

She will light it with candles so the rooms won't look so spare and in need of painting. She'll put a throw on the sofa so no one will see that it is quite tattered. If she had inherited some of her father's money, if Elena had not taken it all, if the courts had seen to accept her contesting of the will, she would have a new sofa. She would have another life.

But this is what she has, and she can make the most of it. A party is a good idea, and she is pleased with the thought of it. She will tell the Romanellis well in advance so they won't be put out. She'll

e Loretta and Patrick, of course. And that nice man from the
dieval history department. And some of her colleagues, though
he rarely sees them. And, of course, Charlie.

As she plans the menu in her head, she sees Loretta in the produce aisle. At first she doesn't recognize her. Loretta looks so small
under the bright lights, against the long case. She is touching mel-
ons, squeezing them, then carefully putting them back. For an
instant, before Andrea knows for sure it is Loretta, she thinks this is
some teenager who works here, putting produce in neat pyramidal
piles on the shelf.

"Loretta," Andrea calls, pushing the overflowing cart her way.
"How are you?"

Loretta looks up, startled. She puts a melon back. "Andrea, how
are you? It's so nice to see you. My God, it's been ages since we've
run into you."

Andrea pauses, dissecting the sentence. For the past eight
months until a few weeks ago Loretta has had her over—to dinner,
to cocktails, for tea. She has called and written. It has not been
about simply running into each other for many months. "Well,"
Andrea says, catching her breath, "I've called . . . perhaps you
haven't gotten my messages."

"You know, we have been so busy. We've been traveling, we've
had guests . . ."

"Oh, I know," Andrea says, "you've been traveling. But you're
back now. I was actually thinking of giving you a call. I'm planning
to have a little party. Just cocktails, maybe next Saturday."

"Oh, how nice." It is then that Patrick arrives, arms laden with
whole-grain bread, cereal, basmati rice. Carbohydrates. What
Andrea imagines Loretta lives on. Plates of them, which she says

she just burns off. "I think we're busy next weekend," Loretta
looking up at Patrick as he drops the bread and pasta into their ca

"Oh yes, next weekend isn't good." They exchange a glance, th
loving, knowing glance of a couple who have perfected a certain art
in communicating, the codes by which they understand each other.

"It would be lovely to see you," Loretta says, "but let me check
my calendar. I know we'll be out of town a day or two. I'll call you
to make a plan when we get back."

Andrea carts her groceries home. She has so much food, she
doesn't know what to do with it, so she calls Charlie and invites
him for dinner. She cooks up some steaks in lime and soy with
boiled potatoes and a salad. She tries not to let her anxiety spill
over. She knows that a few months ago she'd be sharing this dinner
with Loretta. She doubts that Loretta intends to call her. It was just
one of those social things people say so they can back gracefully
away.

Over dinner Andrea says to Charlie, "You know, I don't know
what it is, but Loretta has just dropped me. I know this is silly, but
I think she really has."

Charlie shakes his head. "I told you. She's crazy. Everyone knows
it. She just uses people, then drops them."

"But I thought . . . I believed we were friends."

"I'm sure you aren't the first person to feel this way. Anyway,
she's not normal. You know she's had writer's block ever since her
son got into all that trouble. I think he threatened her. He started
showing up when no one was home. He had a key."

"What happened?"

"You know, I didn't want to say this to you before. But I think he
did things."

"Like what?"

"Like sabotage the house. Throw clothes all over the place, put motor oil in the washing machine. And I heard there was some strange stuff left in jars."

Andrea makes a face. "She's never told me anything."

"Of course not. She never talks about it. Afterward she was afraid of him. She didn't want him in her house, but she hit a dry spell. She'll stay there until she finds somebody new to suck the life out of."

A shiver runs through her. Of course this makes sense. She knows it is true. A woman who can't get along with her own son. What can you expect from her? But she still believes they were close. That they were friends. That they each replaced what the other had lost.

"Well," Charlie says, eating his steak, which is tough, "as long as you didn't tell her anything you wouldn't want the whole world to know."

Andrea shakes her head. "I didn't . . . At least I think I didn't."

"Then you've got nothing to worry about. Just forget about her."

But Andrea can't forget about her. It seems as if Loretta is all she can think about, all she wants to talk about. It's a good night for TV, and after dinner Charlie stretches out on the couch to watch a crime-scene series, then *ER*. On a commercial break in some grueling human drama, Andrea wants to broach the subject with him again. But when she turns to talk to him, Charlie has fallen asleep.

The next day, when she logs on to her e-mail, there is a message waiting for her. "Andrea, are you free this afternoon for tea? L.P." Andrea e-mails back right away: "What time?" All day she thinks about this invitation. It has been so long. Perhaps something happened in Loretta's life. Something that made her need to become very private and solitary, but now she is willing to share it with Andrea.

But when Andrea walks in, three other women are already there—two faculty wives and one adjunct professor in the French department. "I thought we'd have a few friends over," Loretta says, giving Andrea a kiss on the cheek. In the living room there is a pot of tea steeping, and the usual finger sandwiches, and the women in their cashmere sweater sets sit talking about the college, how the budget cuts are affecting everyone. How they think the building of the new gymnasium, though it may attract more students, is a waste for a college of Hartwood's kind. "Do we really need a wrestling team?"

"I can't imagine why."

The women cross and uncross their legs. There is the sound of polyester rubbing in the room. Andrea sits quietly, sipping her tea. She is on the couch in her usual seat and feels as if she is sinking once again. She knows this is one of those paybacks—a little obligation Loretta feels she has to fill.

When she gets back from the tea, Andrea drops Loretta a note in the mail. She thanks her. She says she'd love to have dinner sometime soon. Then she waits. She waits by the phone. She tries to talk to Charlie about this, but he seems to have no patience for it. "I told you what she's like," he says. So one night she calls Robby. "Andrea," he says, "what is it about you? Forget it. You're just trading one obsession for another."

But she cannot forget it. She sits at the window looking down at Loretta's garden. It is now filled with the flowers of spring, and Loretta is out there almost daily. The forsythia, the daffodils, come and go, then tulips. Andrea sees Loretta turning the soil, chasing squirrels away.

The cherry blossoms bloom. The roses begin to bud. In those weeks Andrea relives all her conversations with Loretta. She recalls every meeting and all that was said. Every book lent, every meal shared. She writes angry notes in her head. Envisions phone calls that never occur. She wants to find a way to confront Loretta and say, "What is wrong? What have I done?"

In her mind, Andrea runs over that last afternoon in February again and again. The skating, the hot chocolate. The comment about Loretta's son. Sean. And then Andrea understands. She should not have said his name. Loretta never said Sean's name to her, so she must have wondered how Andrea knew it. This must have troubled her. She must have felt betrayed. Andrea sees that she needs to apologize.

But somehow this doesn't seem like enough. Of course the name of the boy would be mentioned somewhere. People would know it. Andrea cannot understand how their connection, so strongly made, was so easily severed.

Late at night she watches the light in Loretta's studio, the light that is now always on. What is she working on? Some new Gothic thriller, or some heady literary work? Andrea begins having mental conversations with Loretta. If you could just explain to me. Just tell me. What is it, exactly, that I have done?

The next night Andrea goes to her studio. It has been a while since she has been here, but she needs to do something. She should try and paint. The brushes Loretta gave her sit on the paper towel where Andrea left them weeks ago. She picks them up one at a time, touching the sable.

She gazes around at her series. "The House on Shallow Lake." Sixty-six paintings, all different, yet all the same. The last one is dark, almost black. An opaque vision where nothing comes through. She sits on her sofa looking at them. Then she goes to the shelf and retrieves the box the brushes came in. The satin one. She lays them in carefully, one at a time, side by side, then closes the lid. She puts them back on the shelf. Then she knows that she is done.

On a May morning Andrea drives out to the mall. She goes to the stationery store she loves, the one that smells of lilac and candles. Sometimes she comes here just to sniff the wildflower odors. She buys cinnamon candles from time to time.

Now she has come to peruse the cards. Carefully she looks over what they have in stock. A photograph of spring flowers—too sentimental. A Matisse still life—too predictable. A Jackson Pollock abstract—too chaotic. An Al Held black-and-white geometric— too cerebral. None of the cards seems right.

In the end she buys three of them—the Matisse, a Man Ray photograph, and a color photograph of woods and a pond, reminiscent of the woods behind their houses. When she gets home, she puts the three cards on her desk, contemplating them. The Man Ray seems too artsy, but perhaps Loretta would like it. The Matisse is lovely, if clichéd. Perhaps the color photo of the woods is too contrived. A bit of an insult, as if to say, "This is where we first spent time together. Don't you remember?"

None of them satisfy her. Andrea decides instead to work on her note. Like a lover, she believes that each word, each gesture, will make a difference. She begins to compose on scrap paper. The tone must be just right—neither pleading nor accusing. Direct yet apologetic. "I am sure there is something I have done." "Somehow, I am afraid, I have offended you."

She writes, "Dear Loretta, It has been a long time since we have had one of our teas. I really enjoyed them and had come to look forward to our intimate talks. I am not sure why they ended, but I can't help wondering if perhaps I did something . . ."

She scratches that out. It seems too direct. Then she writes, "Loretta, It has been such a busy season. I've had so much to do and even a few trips to New York (a gallery does seem interested!) . . ." Too false.

"Dear Loretta, The summer is almost upon us, and before it slips away, I was wondering if you and Patrick might be free any weekend night . . ."

In the end she returns to her first version. Straightforward. She decides there is nothing to lose. Still, she spends a great deal of time at the post office, fussing over the stamp. There are flags and sports heroes. There is a Langston Hughes stamp, but that seems too self-conscious. Ditto for Willa Cather.

Perhaps one day there will be a Loretta Partlow stamp, Andrea thinks. She can see it. Loretta, head in profile, pencil to her chin. The crooked smile as her eyes take it all in. The furrowed brow and foxy nose. I would like to design that stamp, Andrea thinks.

She tries to imagine millions of Americans licking the Loretta Partlow stamp. Why not? After all, there's a life-size Albert Einstein in front of Madame Tussauds. But that intimate gesture—the licking. No, she cannot imagine the estate of Loretta Partlow ever allowing such a thing.

It would be self-sticking. That's what Loretta's stamp would be. Then Andrea decides on American wildflowers. But which flower? Daises, cardinal flower, columbine? In the end she picks lupine, because she likes the purple color and the way the flower stands straight and tall, as if it is strong and can withstand many things.

After she drops the letter into the mail slot, she tries to retrieve it. Already she knows she has made a mistake. That this is wrong. This heightened importance she has given everything. Certainly it cannot be right. As she slips her hand in the slot, the postal clerk gives her a strange look. "It's done," Andrea says to herself. Then she walks away.

That night Andrea goes to sleep staring at the light from Loretta's window. It shimmers out the back and onto the pond. When Andrea lived in the city, she knew when the subway was coming by the light on the tracks. Along with all the other New Yorkers, she'd peer down dark tunnels, watching for the glow. She wonders why the light from Loretta's studio makes her think of such things—as if by watching it, something or someone will arrive.

When she does not hear back from Loretta in five days, a week, she grows fitful and has trouble sleeping. When she does sleep, she dreams of her father. At first she isn't sure who the man is. His face is vague, without characteristics. A man's profile, a dark road. His face tensed. In all of the dreams a small girl sits at his side. She keeps asking the question "Where are we going, Daddy? Where are we going?" But there is no reply.

In other dreams the little girl is not there. Instead Andrea sees a slip of paper lying beside him in the car. She knows that this slip of paper contains instructions. Directions. A place where he has to be, somewhere they are both going. But in the dream when she finally sees the slip of paper, it is always blank.

A few days later, Andrea finds in her mailbox a stamped postcard with a stamp from Loretta Partlow. Nothing Loretta just slipped into her mailbox. It is a scribbled note saying how she appreciated Andrea's card, how they've been so busy, how she'd love to see Andrea as well and she'll call the first chance she gets.

After that there are no more e-mails or cards. No more dropping off of books. There is an occasional invitation to a cocktail with what Andrea would refer to as Loretta's B list—junior faculty, graduate students, or neighbors. Andrea feels sullied, as if she has had a one-night stand—an intense sexual encounter that, once over, drifts into nothing. A kind of nonrecognition, as if the two people have never shared intimacies at all.

All that remains of what was between them is Loretta's light, which burns into the night like an affront, and Andrea with her desire to smash it.

Eight

In the summer Andrea goes to Assisi, Italy, to teach in a program for American students. She is to instruct her students in how to look. How to see color. Design. In fact, her class is called, rather foolishly, "How to See in Italy." But Andrea likes her students, and she loves driving them in a van around the hill towns.

Charlie was supposed to come with her. They'd first talked about his coming for the whole summer, then a few weeks. Then a long weekend. Somehow, more and more things had come up. The *Hartwood Chronicle* was expanding its alumni relations, adding to its database. It became harder and harder for Charlie to get away. But he agreed to keep her dogs. His e-mails were mainly about his walks with Pablo and Chief.

So Andrea gazes with her students at the crumbling Giottos in the Church of Saint Francis, recently restored. They stand in Siena's main square and draw from all angles. They study three-dimensional objects, including the hill towns themselves, and how they are sited. Andrea talks with them about Leonardo, about Piero della Francesca.

Everything in Italy is about perspective, she tells her students. She shows them the same painting, the same narrow street opening onto a piazza, from half a dozen angles. What is brilliant about Italian artists and architects, what the Renaissance gave us, she says, was their understanding of point of view.

In the afternoons when she is not teaching, she walks the streets of Assisi or whatever town they are visiting. She wishes Charlie had been able to join her. He would have loved to walk these narrow streets, to linger in cafés. But it is Loretta she thinks of most. Sometimes she wants to sit down and write her a postcard, but she keeps wondering if this is the right thing to do. How would Loretta take it? Would she respond? In the end Andrea does. Sends a simple note on a postcard of an Italian landscape. Afterward, as if she can't help herself, she goes into a souvenir shop and finds a Christmas ornament. A Botticelli angel. She thinks it would look beautiful on Loretta's tree.

When she returns to Hartwood, it is late August. She has been away for six weeks, and it feels good to get home. As she sifts through the weeks of mail—mostly third-class solicitations, gallery openings she's missed or shows of friends that will soon open—she realizes she has been expecting something. Hoping for a card, a note from Loretta. An invitation, at least. But nothing awaits her.

A few nights later, she takes Charlie to the French bistro for dinner, to thank him for watching her dogs. He tells her gently, tentatively, that he has been seeing a young woman who works in admissions. "I didn't plan for this to happen, but, well, it just did . . ."

Andrea feels a jab like a needle prick, then nothing at all. As she sips her wine, she feels as if she is floating. This reminds her of drugs. It is not that she doesn't mind. It's that she doesn't seem to feel much. She loves Charlie and has always wanted him to be happy. But that other feeling—in love, whatever that is—has never really happened for her, not with anyone if she thinks about it, but she doesn't want to. She reaches across the table, touches his hands. "It's okay, Charlie. Maybe we're better as friends."

Charlie nods. "I know." And then he adds, "I wish you were furious. I wish you did mind."

"Yes, so do I." It is a warm night, and a breeze blows through the restaurant. She thinks how Charlie has been there for her for so long. How much they've gone through together. Or perhaps how much he went through with her. She will never forget it. "I don't think anyone has ever been so kind to me as you," she tells him.

Charlie smiles, and Andrea knows that this is not enough for him. It never was. They finish dinner rather quickly, and Andrea gets the bill. "This is on me," she says.

"Really, you shouldn't."

"I said I would. I owe you . . . for the dogs."

They walk out together in the night, and she holds his hand. He kisses her on the lips. "You know where to find me." He waits for her to get into her car and drive off. As she does, tears fill her eyes. She wishes she had loved him better. Or more. But she knows as she drives that it wasn't Charlie she thought about over the summer. It wasn't Charlie she wanted to come home to.

Like a song stuck in her head—an earworm, she thinks it's called, the brain searching to fill a void—it's Loretta she can't get of her mind. Andrea feels as if she has gone full circle with her, back to the place where they began a year ago. She recalls weeping in Loretta's kitchen as she sliced an onion. Picking out that yellow watering can. The exchanges of books and knowledge. Doesn't Loretta understand? Why doesn't she see things as Andrea does?

Yet as Andrea's mind churns, aware that something is missing, she is also aware of what is happening. Her life is moving forward in its own way. A gallery in Manhattan has expressed interest in her *House on Shallow Lake* series. The gallery owner called it "a magnificent obsession." There is talk of a show in the spring, and Andrea is focused on making that happen. She has also been assigned an advanced drawing class. Some of her former students—the more talented ones, including Marc and Beth—have signed up again.

She has things to be happy about, Andrea thinks as she pulls into her driveway. The air smells sweet. She glances once at Loretta's house and is surprised to see that it is dark.

For the first class Andrea has set up a still life of chairs, a table, a bowl, a vase, a birdcage. The problem is negative space. "I don't want you to draw the objects. I want you to draw the space around the objects."

The students look at her, confused. One raises his hand. "What is the point of doing that?" he asks, a smirk on his face.

She has become immune to students like this. "Sometimes we see better if we don't look directly at the thing we are drawing but rather at the place it inhabits."

The boy looks back at her blankly. Then he picks up his pencil, as do the rest of them, and begins to draw.

On the way home she stops at the mall. She needs food, some art supplies. A card for Robby's birthday. She enjoys strolling up and down, looking into the shops. She comes to Bookends, a hodge-podge of a bookstore, but they've been able to hold their own with the chains, and she tries to support them.

A poster in the window catches her eye. It is the image that captures her. A man, his eyes open but startled, an odd pleading expression on his face. He is frozen, encased beneath a sheet of ice. A girl dressed in red skates on top of him. The girl is twirling, her face hidden from view. It is a haunting image, and Andrea is struck by it.

Across the top, written in the same red, is the title, *Revenge*. And below that "A riveting new novel by Loretta Partlow." There is a blurb from Sachiko Uni, the famous critic: "In this novel Partlow brings together her flare for the mysterious with her driving story-telling engine, and the result is a page-turning thriller as frightening in its psychology as it is in its surprise ending." And from *Kirkus Reviews:* "This is Partlow at her most complex and compelling. In this novel she has tapped the vein that has eluded her in her last few efforts."

Andrea goes into the store and the owner, who knows her, gives her a nod. She finds the novel in a large stack and takes it into the back of the store, where there is a small café. Instead of ordering, she sits down and reads the jacket copy, which tells of a young woman's antipathy toward her father and her desire to get back at him for abandoning her. She sits motionless for a moment, like someone who has opened the obituaries and seen a familiar face. Then she buys a copy and takes it home.

That night she makes herself a dinner of pasta and wine. When she is done, she washes the dishes and walks the dogs. Then she sits on the couch and begins reading. She knows from the opening lines that this is not recycled Loretta Partlow or, even contrary to what *Kirkus* says, Loretta from long ago. This is not the tired, predictable stories she has been churning out. It is, in fact, something entirely new.

Andrea reads about the farmhouse and the lake. A family of three siblings, the middle child, an embittered girl, angry with her father for leaving her mother. This girl acts out. As a young girl, she is the perfect child—playing the piano beautifully, ice skating, getting straight A's. But underneath she is seething. As an adolescent she gets drunk, gets laid. She does drugs. She doesn't come home.

Andrea slams the book shut and paces around the room. How dare she? How could she? Andrea gazes out the window into a dark void. She has to contain herself from walking over there and pounding on the door. Instead she stands at the window, clutching her fists.

Then she goes back to finish *Revenge*. As Andrea reads on, mesmerized, into the night, her anger subsides into an odd relief. She is not sure how this comes to her, but it does. She understands that she has misread the situation. She did not offend Loretta. Nothing she said about Sean, or anything she did, ever offended her. In fact none of it mattered at all. Nor would it have. Loretta had gotten the story she wanted. It was what she was looking for, and once she had it, she had no further use for Andrea. That was the end of it. That was all.

The details have been altered. The main character, whose

name is now Naomi, is a young violinist with a faltering career. She is small and compact, not unlike Loretta, Andrea thinks. Naomi comes from Wisconsin and has tried but failed to make a career for herself in the East. She has returned home to be near her family in Madison but has fallen in with a bad crowd. She is drinking, sexually promiscuous, as her father drifts further away from her.

Andrea sees herself on every page. Not only in the struggling artist, rejected by her father, who lives on the edge, but in the smallest of gestures—the way Naomi rushes from place to place, the saucerlike green eyes, the Tibetan jacket. Andrea wonders if others will know her as well. How does libel law work? Andrea tries to remember—it's not if you can recognize yourself but if you are recognizable to others.

Andrea skips the chapters on the daughter's drug addiction and promiscuity. She flips through the pages of screaming arguments, which seem to go on much too long. She moves quickly, skimming, until she comes to the scene she is looking for. This is not any scene she has ever described, nothing she's ever told anyone. It is late one night, a cold wintry night, and Naomi has just broken up with her boyfriend—a good man, a trombonist named Chip. They have had an argument—a stupid disagreement, really, not something worth breaking up over, almost an argument for argument's sake. Naomi is always pushing the good men away. It is something she does very well. She goes to a bar, and a man in a leather jacket starts buying her drinks. She has one Scotch, then another. The man wants to take her home. She refuses. They have a fight, a kind of sex tussle in the parking lot. This turns Naomi on, and she says, "Why don't you come home with me?"

His name is Bruce or Bob, not a name Naomi remembers. At her home they have a drink, another Scotch, then they start to fool around. He turns on the TV, smokes a cigarette, then they fool around some more until it gets a little rough. And soon Bruce or Bob is all over Naomi and she can't push him away. He has pinned her down and she feels him pushing against her. Shoving. Tearing her. Then there is the pain, the searing pain. When she wakes up, he is gone.

The next morning she's hungover. And depressed. She takes a Valium, and when that doesn't work, she drinks some more. She drinks until she's about to pass out. Then the novel cuts to another point of view—that of the father, a competent orthopedist who still sees patients. He is a specialist in bones, sports medicine. He has an emergency. A boy with a compound fracture. But in his pocket there is a message. A note he keeps looking at, then putting away. It distracts him, this slip of pink paper his secretary left on his desk. He completes his office hours, his hospital rounds. He goes home, where his wife, who is not Naomi's mother, begs him not to go. "She always does this," the wife says.

"I have to," the father says. "She called me. I have to go."

"Of course you do. It's what she wants."

"She might be in trouble," he says. "Besides, she needs me." The stepmother sighs, shaking her head, as the father gets in his car. "I'll be back soon," he says, driving away. The night is dark, a little foggy. It is not that easy to see, and the road takes turns that surprise him. He is not sure of the way, though he has scribbled down the directions. A rural route. A turn at a crossroads. Drive across a bridge, then turn right. You will come to a town.

The moonlight and his headlights guide him on the country

roads. Already he is feeling drowsy. A warm, tingly sensation moves through his limbs. He is trying to remember if he took his medication before he left. The warmth in his limbs grows as he reaches the crossroads, where he turns right. Following the map, he stays on the road for a mile or two.

The sensation in his limbs heightens, and he knows it is not as it should be. He is a doctor, after all, so he has no doubt. An attack of angina at best, he hopes. Perhaps he can make it to the town, where he can stop for help. He should slow down, but he is racing fast to reach her.

As he approaches the bridge, the pain grows in his chest, an ache he can barely describe, and he speeds up even more. His arms grow numb as he tries to steer, and then he feels the car slipping out of his control, careening off the edge of the bridge, turning, then sliding the other way before it flies off like a bird into space.

Andrea sees the father in the car, unconscious, not from the fall but from the heart attack he has just had. The car filling with water. The paper is still clutched in his hand, but slowly, as he dies, he opens his fist.

Now Andrea can read the slip of paper she has wanted to decipher for so long. She wants it to be a grocery list, something ordinary and banal. *Eggs, cheese, milk.* But it is not, and she has known all along it wouldn't be. "Daddy," the crumpled note in her father's hand reads, "please come and get me."

It is a fall morning and Andrea is getting ready for her walk. Already it is late, almost seven. Her dogs have been fed and are anxious to go, but Andrea wants to wait. She has been sitting up much of the night, watching Loretta's house. Or rather, watching the dark place where Loretta's house sits. Because the house has been dark for weeks now.

Andrea finds herself at the window, staring into the void. But there is nothing there. No light. No place for her eyes to land. She feels as if she could tumble into the abyss before her. Things come back now in snatches. Charlie standing in the doorway, shouting. Scotch in cold glasses. Smoking dope in the car of a man she can barely recall. She almost remembers a phone call.

Loretta did get that right. Her father always coming if she called. But Andrea never intended for him to drive out in the night and get her. She just called to hear his voice, the way she often did. To say he was there and to soothe her as he did when she was troubled, to tell her it would be all right even if it would not. To pay attention to her, as he did, when things were wrong. And the note, neither a grocery list nor a desperate plea, just her address and directions to her house. After all, she had recently moved in. He had never been there before. This is what will haunt her. That he was coming to find her that night.

It had never made sense before. But now, suddenly, it does.

All night she sits motionless, waiting for the light. She sits until she can see Patrick rinsing the dishes as Loretta goes out to stretch. Andrea, whose work thus far has been about repetition, admires their routine. She puts on a jacket and heads out toward the trailhead. As she walks, she prepares what she wants to say to Loretta about the story she has told.

She sees them coming toward her. Kippy racing between them. Loretta hesitates, then stops still. Her finger goes to her chin as if she has forgotten something. She whispers to Patrick. Then they turn around and go back to their house.

But Andrea turns, too, and walks until she intercepts them. "Loretta," Andrea says, her mouth making a little cloud. Breathless, she says, "I was wondering if we could speak." She finds she is trembling. Her hands, her chest. She thinks that if Loretta put her hand there, she would die.

"Oh, Andrea, how are you?" Loretta says. "You know, we are in a bit of a hurry . . ."

"But it won't take a moment. Here, I'll walk with you." Andrea falls in stride beside them. "I was wondering. I just read your new book."

Now Loretta's eyes narrow into the ferret eyes Andrea has seen before. She is shaking her head. "Really, Andrea, you know, it's just a story."

"But it's not, exactly," Andrea says, somewhat confused as she reaches out and touches Loretta on the sleeve. She feels Loretta tug away. Once again Loretta makes that gesture that Andrea has come to associate with her. The cornered animal, not to be touched.

Loretta shakes her off and then, for a moment, before she turns, just stares, and it occurs to Andrea as she is standing there that Loretta doesn't see her. She doesn't see her at all.

Nine

Dear Editor:

I have read with interest both your review of *Revenge*, by Loretta Partlow, and the interview you ran in your magazine section. I was struck when your reviewer referred to this novel as "perhaps Partlow's most highly imagined, most fiercely conceived." And by what she herself says in an interview, "It is a story I've had in my head for many years. As with all my novels, this one is a composite of many things—no single one being the true story, or an accurate rendering of anyone or anything."

I am afraid I must take exception with both statements. While Ms. Partlow may well be a novelist of some talent and imagination, this particular story was not hers to tell. It did not belong to her. Rather, it is my story—one I shared with her, it is true, but in confidence, believing that she would respect the boundaries of our friendship. Of course, she has altered the details. I am a painter, not a violinist (though my friend Natalie, whom Ms. Partlow met, is a violinist with long white fingers), and my name isn't Naomi, though I believe the description of the "round-faced girl with the green saucer eyes" is me.

You see, she is my neighbor. Even as I write this, I can see the window of her office, the desk where she writes. I know when she is sitting there, when she is working, when she is pacing. I see her shadow as it moves along the wall. And I know that the story she wrote was hardly imagined or thought of over many years, because it is the story I began to divulge to her only last year."

Does a writer have the right to take whatever story has been handed to her and retell it as if it was hers? Or worse, distort it in unspeakable ways? I am hoping you will publish this, if only to set the record straight.

The story she told is mine. It belongs to me and my family. What happened to us was private. So you see, what Loretta Partlow accomplished has nothing to do with her great narrative drive or her imagination. This novel is about the failure of imagination. It is about usurpation, appropriation. I am an occupied territory. I know what plagiarism is. It refers to the written word. I know that a legal case can be made for the theft of the written word. But what about a person's soul? Can a writer plagiarize a life? Shouldn't there be a law to protect us from that?

Sincerely yours,

Andrea Geller

Adjunct Professor of Visual Arts

Hartwood College, Hartwood Springs, New York

———

When Andrea finishes the letter, she puts it in an envelope but hesitates before putting a stamp on it. She leaves it on her dresser for a few days, then files it in the drawer where she keeps other important things—the documents, the autopsy report, all the notes and cards she has received from Loretta over the past year.

Then she sits at the window. She needs time to think, to plan her next move. She waits as the day turns to dusk, and she sees Patrick go into the kitchen to pour two glasses of wine. Loretta joins him, and they sit at the kitchen table, a yellow pad between them.

Andrea can just imagine what they are saying. "Whom shall we have?" Loretta asks Patrick. "Let's see, there are the Adlers, and Gil and Lila. We have to have them."

"Yes, I suppose so." Patrick nods as they scribble down names. They will do it as they always do. Thirty, forty people. The usual olives, platters of cheese. They will pick up some frozen appetizers from Gourmet to Go. Cheese puffs and mushroom caps. And Loretta will make her watercress sandwiches, which are always a big hit, and Patrick will do the salmon roll.

It is always a simple affair. From six to eight. They will call student catering to get a student to serve.

They've agreed upon the Adlers, who are always entertaining with a large group. And the Markens, who had them for dinner in July, and they never had them back. They'll have the Vitales, and Doug Tramer, who, though he is boring, would be hurt if he's not included.

"What about Andrea?" Patrick says.

"Who?" Loretta asks, distracted, tapping with her pencil.

"Andrea, you know, our neighbor."

"Oh," Loretta says, "I don't think so. Not this time."

The cars are parked in front of Loretta's house and there is a party going on. Perhaps for some visiting dignitary, a Nobel laureate. A Czech writer who happens to be in town. Andrea sees a young man she hasn't seen before. She wonders if he is a new junior faculty member. She tries to determine if there's a resemblance. Is it the prodigal son, returned?

Normally Andrea would sit watching the scene unfold. The comings and goings. Seeing who has been included and who has not. But tonight she doesn't bother. She is busy packing, sorting through her things, tossing out what she doesn't need. She can fit most of her belongings into her car, and she is determined to do it in one load. Mrs. Romanelli is sorry she is leaving. She's been a good tenant, always considerate, paying her rent on time. And it has been nice for Mrs. Romanelli to have a young woman in the house.

But Andrea has taken a small apartment in faculty housing, where Natalie lives. She will stay there a year before moving on. Jim Adler has told her that her appointment will not be renewed. Something about terminal contracts—an expression that disturbed her. He said, "This is your terminal contract."

He tried to ease the blow. All junior faculty who had been at the college a certain number of years, including Natalie, would not be rehired. Andrea was not to take it personally. But of course she has, though she tries not to. Anyway, she has other things to do. Her *House on Shallow Lake* series has been completed. There are now almost fifty small paintings, less the one she sold to Loretta, and the gallery in Chelsea is now set to show them in the spring. She has taken the sable brushes down from the shelf. She has plans to use them again.

She is ready to move on. Robby was glad when he heard. "Good for you, Andrea. Really, God knows, it's time."

It is just dawn when the car is packed. Andrea gets in with her dogs, ready to leave. But instead of driving out of Hartwood Springs, she heads down to the dead end where Loretta's house—that spider weaving its web—with all its extensions and wings, sits. It is too early for them to be up, especially after their party the night before. Still, Andrea approaches slowly.

Pulling up in front, she admires their garden for the last time. Loretta has added some new varieties of mums, and the fall clematis has really established itself. It climbs all over the back trellis. The garden is a lush, beautiful sight.

Andrea gets out of her car, careful not to let her door slam, and stands in front of Loretta's house. She thinks how she misses sitting in the blue living room that reminded her of heaven, looking out at all of this. How she'd come to feel at home here. But she will capture it. Hold on to what she remembers. A part of it will remain hers.

Andrea takes a small camera out of her pocket. A disposable. She takes one snapshot of the house. Then she gets in her car and drives away.

Acknowledgments

I would like to thank Michael Cunningham, Valerie Martin, Peter Orner, Dani Shapiro, and Susan Shreve for their thoughtful readings and editorial advice. Josh Dorman for his help in researching Andrea as an artist and for sharing with me some of his teaching ideas. I want to thank Ellen Levine, as always, for her enormous support and impeccable judgment, and Diane Higgins whose focused readings and patient explanations strengthened this work in so many ways. Nichole Argyres whose enthusiasm and attention to details have made the production of this book a pleasure. To my family and friends who have been there, always. And Larry O'Connor, whose devotion to language and to this book, was astonishing, but came as no surprise.